CORY DOCTOROW

Winner of the John W. Campbell Award
Locus Award
Sunburst Award
Electronic Frontier Foundation Pioneer Award
Prometheus Award
White Pine Award

"Doctorow uses science fiction as a kind of cultural WD-40, loosening hinges and dissolving adhesions to peer into some of society's unlighted corners."
—*New York Times*

"Doctorow demonstrates how memorably the outrageous and the everyday can coexist."
—*Publishers Weekly*

"Doctorow shows us life from the point-of-view of the plugged-in generation and makes it feel like a totally alien world."
—*Montreal Gazette*

He's got the modern world, in all its Googled, Friend-stered and PDA-d glory, completely sussed.
—*Kirkus Reviews*

PM PRESS OUTSPOKEN AUTHORS SERIES

THE GREAT BIG BEAUTIFUL TOMORROW

plus . . .

THE GREAT
BIG BEAUTIFUL
TOMORROW

plus
"Creativity vs. Copyright"
and
"Look for the Lake"
Outspoken Interview

CORY DOCTOROW

PM PRESS | 2011

This edition © 2011 PM Press

Series Editor: Terry Bisson

ISBN: 978-1-60486-404-5
LCCN: 2011927947

PM Press
P.O. Box 23912
Oakland, CA 94623
PMPress.org

Printed in the USA on recycled paper, by the Employee
Owners of Thomson-Shore in Dexter, Michigan.
www.thomsonshore.com

Outsides: John Yates/Stealworks.com
Insides: Josh MacPhee/Justseeds.org

CONTENTS

THE GREAT BIG
BEAUTIFUL TOMORROW

PART 1: A SPARKLING JEWEL

I PILOTED THE MECHA THROUGH the streets of Detroit, hunting wumpuses. The mecha was a relic of the Mecha Wars, when the nation tore itself to shreds with lethal robots, and it had the weird, swirling lines of all evolutionary tech, channeled and chopped and counterweighted like some freak dinosaur or a racecar.

I loved the mecha. It wasn't fast, but it had a fantastic ride, a kind of wobbly strut that was surprisingly comfortable and let me keep the big fore and aft guns on any target I chose, the sights gliding along on a perfect level even as the neck rocked from side to side.

The pack loved the mecha too. All six of them, three aerial bots shaped like bats, two ground-cover streaks that nipped around my heels, and a flea that bounded over buildings, bouncing off the walls and leaping from monorail track to rusting hover-bus to balcony and back. The pack's brains were back in Dad's house, in the old Comerica Park site. When I found them, they'd been a pack of sick dogs, dragging themselves through the ruined city, poisoned by some old materiel. I had done them the mercy of extracting their brains and connecting them up to the house network. Now they were immortal, just like me, and they knew that I was their alpha dog. They loved to go for walks with me.

I spotted the wumpus by the plume of dust it kicked up. It was well inside the perimeter, gnawing at the corner of an old satellite Ford factory, a building gone to magnificent ruin, all crumbled walls and crazy, unsprung machines. The structural pillars stuck up all around it, like columns around a Greek temple.

The wumpus had the classic look. It stood about eight feet tall, with a hundred mouths on the ends of whipping tentacles. Its metallic finish was smeared with oily rainbows that wobbled as the dust swirled around it. The mouths whipped back and forth against the corner of the factory, taking chunks out of it. The chunks went into the hopper on its back and were broken up into their constituent atoms, reassembled into handy, safe, rich soil, and then ejected in a vertical plume that was visible even from several blocks away.

Wumpuses don't put up much fight. They're reclamation drones, not hunter-killer bots, and their main mode of attack was to assemble copies of themselves out of dead buildings faster than I could squash them. They weren't much sport, but that was OK: there's no *way* Dad would let me put his precious mecha at risk against any kind of big game. The pack loved hunting wumpus, anyway.

The air-drones swooped around it in tight arcs. They were usually piloted by Pepe, the hysterical chihuahua, who loved to have three points-of-view, it fit right in with his distracted, hyperactive approach to life. The wumpus didn't even notice the drones until one of them came in so low that it tore through the tentacles, taking three clean off and disordering the remainder. The other air-drones did victory loops in the sky overhead, and the flea bounded so high that it practically disappeared from sight, then touched down right next to the wumpus.

This attack was characteristic of Gretl, the Irish Setter mix who thought she was a kangaroo. The whole pack liked the flea, but Gretl was born to it. She bounced the wumpus six times, knocking it back and forth like an air-hockey puck, leaping free before it could bring its tentacles to bear on her.

The ground-effect bots reached the wumpus at the same time as I did. Technically, I was supposed to hang back out of range and get it with the mecha's big guns, to make sure that it didn't get a bite or two in on the mecha's skin, scratching the finish. But that was *no fun at all*. I liked to dance with the wumpus, especially when the pack was in on it, all of us dodging in and out, snatching the wumpus's tentacles, kicking it back and forth. The ground-effect bots were clearly piloted by Ike and Mike, two dogs that had been so badly mutilated when I found them that I couldn't even guess at their breed. They must have been big beasts at one point. They were born to ground-effect bots, anyway, bulling the wumpus around.

The wumpus was down to just a few tentacles now, and I could see into its hopper, normally obscured by the forest of waving arms and mouths. The hopper itself was lined with tentacles, but thin ones, whiplike, each one fringed with hairy cilia. The cilia branched and branched again, down to single-molecule pincers, each one optimized to break apart a different kind of material. I knew better than to reach inside that hopper with the mecha's fists—even after I'd killed the wumpus, the hopper would digest anything I fed it, including me.

Its foot-spoked wheels spun madly as we batted it around like a cat playing with a mouse. They could get traction on anything, given enough time to get their balance, but we weren't going to give it the chance. The air-drones snipped the last of the tentacles, and I touched the control that whistled the pack back. They obediently came to my heels, and I put the wumpus in my sights. The wumpus seemed to sense what was coming. It stopped struggling and settled down on the feet of its wheels. I methodically blew apart its hopper with my depleted uranium guns, chipping away at it, blowing it open, cilia waving and spasming. Now the wumpus was just a coil of metallic skin and logic with a hundred wheels, naked and stripped. I used the rocket-launcher on it and savored the debris-fountain that rose from it. Sweet!

"Jimmy Yensid, you are cruel and vile!" The voice bounced off the walls of the ruined buildings around me, strident and shrill. I rotated the mecha's cowl and scanned the ground. There she was, standing on top of a dead hover-bus, a spidergoat behind her on a tether. I popped the cowl and shinned down the mecha, using the grippy hand- and toe-holds that tried to conform to my grasp.

"Hello, Lacey!" I called. "You're looking very pretty today." Dad had always taught me to talk to girls this way, though there weren't many meat girls in my world, just the ones I saw online and, of course, the intriguing women of the Carousel of Progress, back in the center of Comerica Park. And it was true. Lacey Treehugger was ever so pretty—with a face as round as a pie-plate and lips like a drawn-up bow. Talking to Lacey was as forbidden as destroying the mecha, maybe more, but Dad could tell if the mecha got scratched and he had no way of finding out if I had been passing the time of day with pretty Lacey.

She was taller than me now, which was only to be ex-pected, because she was not immortal and so she was grow-ing at regular speed while I was going to stick to my present, neat little size for a good while yet. I didn't mind that she was taller, either—I liked the view.

"Hello, hello," I said as I scaled the hover, coming up to stand next to her. "Hello!" I said to the spider-goat, hold-ing out the flat of my hand for it to sniff. It brayed at me and menaced me with its horns. "Come on, Louisa, play nice."

She tugged on the goat's lead, a zizzing spool of some-thing that felt as soft as felt but could selectively tighten at the loop-end when the goat got a little too edgy. "This *isn't*

Louisa, Jimmy. This is Moldavia. Louisa died last week." She glared at me.

"I'm sorry to hear it," I said. "She was a good goat."

"She died from eating bad sludge," Lacey said. Ah. Well, that explained it. Lacey's people hated Dad's preserve here in the old city of Detroit. They hadn't made the wumpuses, but they fully supported their work. The Treehuggers wanted all of the old industrial world converted back to the kind of thing you could let a goat eat without worrying about it dropping dead, turning to plastic, or everting its digestive tract.

"You should keep a closer eye on your goats, Lacey," I said. "It's not safe for them to wander around here."

"It *would be* if you'd leave off hunting those innocent wumpuses. The way you took that poor thing apart, it was sickening."

"Lacey, it's a *machine*. It doesn't have feelings. I was just having a little fun."

"Sickening," she repeated. She had her short hair in tiny braids today, which is one of the many ways I loved to see it. Each braid was tipped with a tiny, glittering bead of fused soil, stuff that her people collected as a reminder of the bad old days.

"How's your parents?"

She didn't manage to hide her smile. "Their weirdness is terminal. This week they decided that we were going to try to sell spider-goat silk to India. I'm all like, India? Are you crazy? What does India want with our textiles? They don't even *need* clothes there anymore, not since desidotis came out." Desidotis were self-cleaning, self-replicating, and could reconfigure themselves. No one who made dollars could afford them—they were denominated in rupees only. "And they went, have you *seen* how the rupee is trading today? So they're all over iBay, posting auction listings in broken Hindi. I'm all like, you *know* that India is the world's largest English-speaking nation, right?"

I shook my head. "You're right. Terminally weird."

She gave me a playful shove. "You're one to talk. At least mine are human!"

So technically it was true. Dad refused to call himself a human anymore. Ever since he attained immortality, decades before I was born, he'd called himself a transhuman. But when he said he wasn't human, it was a boast. When Lacey said it, it sounded like an insult. It bugged me. Dad didn't want me "deracinating" myself with Lacey. Lacey didn't trust me because I wasn't a "real" human. It wasn't like I wanted to be a mayfly, like the Treehuggers were, but I still hated it when Lacey looked down her nose at me.

"I really do hate the way you take those wumpuses apart," she said. "It gives me the creeps. I know they're not alive, but you really seem to be enjoying it."

"The pack enjoys it," I said, gesturing at my robots, who were wrestling each other around my feet. "It's in their nature to hunt."

She looked away. "I don't like them, either," she said, barely above a whisper.

"Come on," I said. "They're better off now than they were when I found them. At least I haven't screwed around with their germ plasm. I'm just using technology to let them be better dogs. Not like Louisa there." I pointed to the spider-goat.

"Moldavia," she said.

I knew I had her there. I pressed my advantage. "You think she enjoys giving silk? Somewhere in her head, she knows she's supposed to be full of milk."

Lacey looked out over the ruins of Detroit. "Pretty around here," she said.

"Yeah," I said. It was. The ruins were glorious. They were all I'd ever known, except for flyovers in the zepp. Michigan countryside was pastoral and picturesque, but it wasn't anything so magnificent as Detroit's ruins. So much ambition. Made me proud to be (trans)human. "I wish you guys would stop trying to take it away from us."

This is how conversation with Lacey always went, each of us picking fights with the other. It was all we knew, the best way we had to relate. Neither of us really meant it. It was just an excuse to stand close enough to her to count the hairs on her arms, to watch the sun through her eyelashes.

She looked at me. "It's not like you let anyone else come by and see it anyway. You just hoard it all to yourself."

"You come by whenever you want. What's the problem?"

"You treat it like your own private playground. You know how many people could live here?"

"None," I said. "It would kill them within a week." I was immune, thanks to my transhuman liver. Dad's liver wasn't quite so trick, but he made do by eating cultured yogurt filled with microbes that kept him detoxed. He said it was a small price to pay for continued residence in his museum.

"You *know* what I mean," she said, socking me again. "Let the wumpuses do their thing, turn this whole place back into forests, grow some treehouses . . . How many? A million? Two million?"

"Sure," I said. "Provided you didn't care about destroying all this history."

"There are billions of blown-out steel-belted radials!" she said. "All over the world. What the hell makes yours so special?"

"What if this was ancient Rome?" I said. "What if we were all sitting around, thinking about pounding down all those potsherds, and you were all like, Jimmius Yensidus, what are you saving all those potsherds for? Rome is full of them. They're a health hazard! The centurions keep cutting their feet on them!"

"You are a total idiot," she said.

We got to this point in every discussion. Half the time, I called her an idiot. Half the time it was the other way around. We sat down on the bus and she put her arm around me. I leaned in for my kiss. Dad would totally splode if he knew. Deracination!

Sorry, Dad. She kissed me slowly, with a lazy bit of tongue that made the hair on my neck stand up. She was probably getting a little old for me, but I found that I quite liked older women.

She broke it off and sighed. "You're so young," she said. "We can't keep doing this."

"I'm two months older than you," I said, baiting her. I knew what she meant.

"You used to be. These days, it's like you're ten. I'm almost fourteen, Jimmy."

"So go kiss some Treehugger boys on the spider-goat farm," I said.

She sighed again. "Are you really happy here?"

"Are you happy where you are?"

"I'm happy enough. It's peaceful."

"Boring."

"Yeah," she said.

"It's not boring around here. Going out with Dad is *awesome*." Dad collected pieces for his museum from all over the world. We'd gone to France together the year before to get the Girl and the Sultan's Elephant from Marseilles. The semirobotic puppets were eleven meters tall and we'd stashed them in a high-school gym near the bus station. We couldn't work them on our own, they needed a crew of twenty or more, but I was working on training the pack to help out. Trying, anyway. Pepe kept trying to eat the Elephant.

"But you're all *alone*. And your dad is so *weird*."

"He's weird, but he's a lot of fun. I won't live here forever, anyway. Once I'm post-pube, I'm going on a vision-quest. It's part of the package. Then I'll find somewhere to settle down."

"You've got it all figured out, huh?"

Pepe had been circling high overhead as we chatted, occasionally dipping down to play with the ground-effect critters. Now all three of his drones lofted high, making wide circles. That was the signal that he was seriously freaking out.

I stood up to get a better look at him, Lacey grabbing at my hand. I followed the wide, swooping curves of the drones, turning to watch, and saw two of them get shot out of the sky, one-two, just like that, disappearing in a hail of debris.

Lacey squeezed my hand.

"Kurzweil on a crutch," I breathed. I headed for the mecha, but Lacey wouldn't let go of my hand. "Come on," I said, looking into her scared face. "You ride shotgun, I'll get you home safe." She shook her head. Her eyes were white. The pack was going crazy around us, nipping at our heels, racing in circles. The flea was springing high, high, higher. The crack of artillery. A flight of rockets screamed overhead, then touched down somewhere. The sound was incredible, like nothing I'd ever heard, and the earth shook so hard that I slipped and went down on one knee.

"Come *on*," I said to Lacey, "get in!"

I grabbed for the bottom rung of the mecha's handholds and felt it grip me back. I looked over my shoulder. Lacey was hugging the goat. Dammit. The goat.

"We'll take her too!" I said. I reached for the goat, but she butted at me and shied back. "Lacey, you can't stay here," I said. There was the rattle of small arms, another volley of rockets. A cloud of dust boiled down the street. I barely managed to yank my shirt over my head before it overtook us, blotting out the sky, filling every pore with grey, shattered concrete. It was like a wumpus plume gone metastatic, filling the entire world.

I tugged my shirt back into place and looked around. Lacey was gone.

I jumped down from the hover and ran around the bus. The pack were everywhere around me. I tried to whistle them up and send them in a search pattern for Lacey and the goat, but I needed the mecha for that.

I wasn't thinking straight.

I turned and crouched down and put my face in my hands and breathed deeply. Then I stood up, thumped the ground-effect critters behind the ears, and climbed into the mecha and sealed the cowl, turning on air, radiation, and flash-bang filters at max. The screens were all going bonkers. I took another deep breath. First things first. Pepe was still up there. I dropped his sensorium on the side-screens, dialed back to when he first started to circle, absently watching the attacks unfold.

On the main screens, I put up the view from the ground effects and the flea, and told them to fan out and look for Lacey. Pepe had been watching the attack when Lacey went missing, so his rewind wasn't any help there, but at least I could watch the attack that had unfolded.

There were eight mechas in formation, coming across the river from where Windsor used to be. It was our least-guarded flank—we counted on the river as the first line of defense. If I was planning an invasion, that's where I'd strike, too.

The mechas were smaller than mine. They were barely bigger than their pilots, more powered armor than vehicles. I recognized them as coming from the earliest years of the Mecha Wars, whereas my mecha was the last generation produced, a juggernaut that stood four times larger than them. The pack hadn't found Lacey. I looked at the screens and decided that Lacey had gone to ground somewhere, hiding in a ruined building. Fine. She'd be as safe there as she was anywhere. I began to run for Windsor.

o o o

Dad wouldn't answer his phone. I dropped mine into the mecha's hopper and told it to keep on redialing him. It kept getting the voicemail: "You have reached Robin Yensid and the Detroit Conservation Zone. We are delighted to hear from another telephone user. Your choice of communications technology is appreciated. Help keep the telephone alive! That said, I can't come to my phone right now. Leave me a message and I'll phone you back."

My mecha ran full tilt, bent almost double. The cockpit remained level on the end of the mecha's flexible stalk of a neck, rolling silently from side to side to keep from upsetting me. It didn't even spill my coffee.

Who'd be attacking Detroit? Dad believed that the wumpuses were made by some kind of co-op in San Diego, deep greens who'd made the viral bots and released them into the wild more than ten years ago. I'd checked out the co-op's presence a couple times and it was mostly arguments about who was supposed to be tucking the oxen into bed each night, and what kinds of stories were appropriate to read to the calves. Apparently, the co-op had changed focus after their wumpus phase and had gone into farming. In any event, I didn't think that they were the kind of gang that could send eight members across the continent in mechas to make sure that the last real city got ploughed under by wumpuses.

The mecha told me that it had the eight enemy craft in range of its missiles. I stopped and dropped the third leg for stability and sighted on the flank closest to me. I thought I'd pick them off in order, closest to furthest, and hope that the far ones wouldn't even notice what I was up to until I'd already done it.

I told the missile which mecha to attack—it was purple, and Pepe's imaging showed a driver behind the cowl that was about Dad's size, though I couldn't tell sex or age. I put my finger over the button and got ready to press it. But I didn't push the button.

I had killed a million wumpuses. I'd put some dogs out of their misery, beasts too far gone to join the pack. I'd swatted flies and sploded mosquitoes with lasers. But I'd never killed a human being. Technically, I was a transhuman, so was that still murder? My thumb thought so.

Dad's voicemail came up again. The mecha closest to me was swiveling toward me. I could hear its radar scattering off my armor. I hit the button and my mecha rocked as the rocket screamed away from the frame on my mecha's chest. The missile corkscrewed through a tracker-confounding set of spirals, shaking off radar chaff as it went. The chaff was propelled as well, and it, too, moved through corkscrews, so that even *I* couldn't figure out which was the real missile and which were the drones.

Then, the moment of contact.

The real missile hit the mecha dead center. I watched its nose-cam as it kissed the chest-plate, seeing the mouth of the man (woman?) inside, shot up through the clear shield. The mouth made a perfect O. Then the chest-cam stopped working. I looked out with my naked eyes in time to see the mecha come apart in an expanding cloud of debris. Not all the debris was made of metal. There was a red mist in the air. Something wet hit the ground. It must have been part of a person, once, but now it looked like roadkill. Like the dogs that couldn't make it into the pack.

I was a murderer. The person in that mecha might have been an immortal like me. Or she might have been made into an immortal, like Dad. Might have lived forever.

The other mechas were targeting me now, three moving to flank me, two grasping forearms and locking at the ankles to make a single unit, which rose into the air on rotors over their shoulders.

I had already armed the remaining missiles and targeted the four closest to me without even thinking of it. I played a lot of mecha sims on slow days, sometimes using the console in front of the huge, chunky TV in the living room of the fourth scene of the Carousel of Progress. Dad did not approve of this, so I didn't tell him.

I launched the battery and used the recoil time to bring the evaders up to nominal. This was the mecha's gymnastics program, a set of heavily randomized backsprings and twirls and such, supposedly impossible for a targeting system to get a lock on, but nevertheless calculated to keep the enemy in range at all times. Theoretically, the brave pilot (ahem, me) could continue to harass and kill the enemy while pulling four gees through a set of acrobat maneuvers. The evaders were better than the carny rides Dad kept refurbished and running, but truth be told, they'd never failed to make me puke.

But as the missiles screamed toward the enemy mechas and the airborne unit bore down on me, big guns blazing, puking seemed like a sensible alternative to dying. I hit the evaders and dug in.

I'd ridden the evaders dozens of times, but this was the first time I kept my eyes open. The nausea didn't rush up and overtake me. Instead, I remained utterly focused on the enemy craft, my gaze locked on them as my body rocked and flipped. My missiles had taken down two more, the other missiles had disappeared, either foiled by antitargeting systems or knocked out of the sky.

I threw more bad stuff in their direction, using the conventional depleted uranium rounds as the flips and turns brought me into range. The evaders were hard on the mecha's power-cells, so the maneuvers only ran for a few minutes, but it felt like hours. When we ground to a halt, my mecha and I, we were much closer to the enemy craft than before. There had been eight of them. Now there were three. The two that had taken to the sky were lying in a twisted wreckage near me.

The pack were barking like crazy, filling the cockpit with alerts. The flea was bouncing up and down on the downed aerial unit, savaging the pilots through their cowls. It kept replaying its video of the kill, the flea leaping up to land on the rotors' mast, biting down on the drive-shaft and hanging on as the rotors bent, collided, spun away, the flea bounding free of the dying craft as it spun out and spiraled down.

The remaining mecha were moving with more discipline and purpose than their brethren had. I no longer had the advantage of surprise. These three were taking cover behind Dad's favorite office tower, a big white marble thing done in a style Dad called "deco." They lobbed missiles over the building, apparently using orbitals or something stratospheric for targeting.

Two could play at that game. I whistled up the flea and Pepe and sent them around the back of the tower, giving me some guidance for my own targeting systems. My mecha knew well enough to automatically interface with the lads, tying them straight into its guidance systems. I fired some grenades at the parking structure opposite their covering building, letting the mecha calculate the bank shot so that they bounced off and landed amid the enemies.

Two more down, and the other two were on the move, streaking out from behind the building. Holy crap, they were *fast*. They fired in unison at me, letting me have it with guided missiles, grenades, conventional ammo. I tried evasive maneuvers but it was no good. They shot the mecha's left leg out from under it and I tumbled . . .

. . . and kept rolling. The Mecha Wars were vicious, and once a ronin mecha was in the field, it might go months without a resupply or maintenance. These bastards kept coming at you no matter what, pulling themselves along on whatever limbs were left, until there was nothing left to fight with.

My mecha came up in a three-pointed stance, like one of the ground-effect vehicles, like it was doing yoga, coming into a downward dog. The cowl swung around and I was upright again, atop the thorax of my newly bug-like fighting machine.

The ground-effect puppies nipped at my heels as I scuttled toward the enemy, closing. I was down to nothing but conventional ammo now, so it was close fighting. In a pinch, my mecha could uproot a building and clobber them with it. Two minutes before, I'd been agonizing about becoming a murderer. Now I wanted to tear their legs off and beat them to death with them.

The dogs wanted to do their thing and I gave them the nod over my command channel. The entire pack converged on one of the two mechas—the closer one—grabbing its limbs and tumbling it to the ground, rending the metal away from the cowl. I actually heard the pilot scream. It made me grin.

That left one more. He—it was a he, I was close enough to see that now—he had planted himself in a fencer's stance, presenting the side of his body to me as he raised his near hand straight out toward me, the maws of his guns yawning toward me. His other arm was curled across his chest, fanning up and down, trying to keep me in his sights at all times.

I scuttled my mecha forward, taking cover when I could, using trucks and houses, even a beautiful neon sign that Dad always stopped to admire when we were out for walks. It sploded and came down with a series of crystal tinkling noises.

I got as many shots off at it as I could, but it was fresh, with a seemingly endless supply of ammo to harry me with whenever I tried to target it.

Then it got me, bouncing a grenade off the ground ten yards ahead of me, sending it sailing right into the mecha's midsection, so that I flipped and rolled and rolled and rolled. *Now* I felt nauseated.

When I finally stopped rolling, I knew I was about to die. The mecha's lights were all dark, all systems down. Dad was going to *kill* me. I chuckled and groaned. My ribs, pressed into the crash harness, felt like a handful of dried twigs rattling against one another.

I struggled to release the webbing as I punched the trigger for the charges that blew out the cowl. I would die on my feet.

I got out of the mecha just in time to see the ground-effect puppies streaking toward the enemy mecha, who was raising his guns for the triumphant kill. I saw in an instant what they intended, and turned my face away just as they collided with him, exploding in a shower of hot metal. I dived back into the cowl, heedless of my ribs, and curled into a ball as the debris rained down around me.

When I straightened up, the remaining mecha was a twisted, blackened wreck, streaked with red. The two doggies had gone into suicide-bomber mode when they saw that my life was endangered, blowing themselves up and taking the remaining enemy with them. Good doggies. When I got back home, I'd give their brains some extra endorphins. They'd earned it. Of course, finding them some more bots to pilot wasn't going to be easy. Dad's museum-city was cratered with the aftermath of my battle, buildings razed, fires blazing.

I took a tentative step away from the wreckage of my mecha and stumbled, gasping at the pain in my ribs. Then I remembered that I'd left my phone in the cockpit and had to crawl back in to get it. It was still redialing Dad, still getting his voicemail.

A part of my brain knew that this meant that he was in deep trouble, somewhere in Detroit. That part seemed to be locked in a padded room, judging by its muffled cries. The part in charge didn't worry about Dad at all—Dad was fine, he was back at Comerica, waiting for me. He was going to be so *pissed* about the mecha. It was the last of its kind, as Dad never tired of reminding me. And several of his favorite buildings were in ruin. This was going to be ugly.

I pocketed the phone and whistled up the pack. It was just the flea and Pepe now. Pepe perched on the flea's shoulder and let me pet his carapace. I tested my legs. Wobbly, but serviceable. Without the mecha, it'd be harder to talk to the pack, but they'd be OK on their own. They had good instincts, my pups.

Normally, it was a ten-minute walk from the Ambassador Bridge to Comerica. Hell, the People Mover monorail went most of the way. But I could see a PeopleMover from where I stood, and it was stock-still, motionless on the track. Someone had cut its power. I took some tentative steps. My ribs grated and I gasped and nearly fell over. The flea bounced to me and nuzzled at me. I leaned on it and it trundled forward slowly. This was going to take a lot more than ten minutes. If only Dad would pick up the phone, he could come and get me.

○ ○ ○

We were halfway to Comerica when my phone rang.

"Dad?"

"Jimmy, thank God. Are you OK?"

I had been very brave all the way from the wreckage, biting back my whimpers of pain and soldiering on. But now I couldn't stop my tears. "I broke my ribs, Dad," I said, around the sobs. "It hurts."

"Where are you?"

"I'm almost home," I said. "Can you come get me?"

"Jimmy, listen carefully. I—" there was a crash on the other end of the phone. It continued rumbling, and I realized I was hearing it with my other ear as well. I looked out over the city and saw Dad's harrier screaming around in a tight arc that must have pulled eight gees. The last time he'd taken the harrier out, I'd been a little kid, only five or six, and he'd flown it like it was made of eggshell. Now it was zipping around like an overclocked Pepe.

The harrier was circling something I couldn't see, and it had all its guns blazing. Dad was knocking the holy hell out of his city, and somehow that made things scarier than ever. He *never* would have—

"Listen carefully, Jimmy! Go home. Get in the zepp. Go away from here. I'll find you. Do you—" the harrier made another tight turn. Something huge was over it, in the sky. A flying battle-platform? I'd seen pictures of those. They'd been big in Europe, during the Mecha Wars. I'd never seen one in person. I didn't think they'd made it to this continent.

"Dad?"

The harrier zigged and zagged like a dragonfly, then rocketed straight up, guns still blazing, rolling from side to side as it laid down a line of fire over the batteries slung under the platform's belly. The platform returned fire, and Dad's voice rang out of the phone: "*Go!*"

I went. My ribs had stiffened up as I watched the air battle, but I pushed on. I didn't worry about crying out when they hurt. I screamed the whole way. I couldn't hear myself over the noise of the guns. The flea kept me upright. Somehow, I made it home.

Comerica's doors were shut up tight, the security scanners live and swiveling to follow me. They were wide-angle and could follow me without moving an inch, but the swiveling let you know they were live. Each one had a pain-ray beneath it, aperture as wide as the muzzle of a blunderbuss. I once came home without my transponder—left in the mecha, in the old car-barn—and got a faceful of pain-ray. Felt like my face was melting. I never forgot my transponder again.

For a second, though, I couldn't find it and I had a vision of it sitting in the wrecked cockpit of my mecha, a ten-minute walk away that might as well have been in one of the moon colonies. Then I found it, transferred absently to one of the many pockets that ran down the sleeves of my sweater.

I let myself in and collapsed in the vestibule, on one of Dad's live divans. It purred and cuddled me, which set my ribs afire again. On the other side of the dome there was a model room for a robot hotel that Dad had rescued from Atlantic City. It had a robutler that could do rudimentary first aid. I'd grown up playing hospital with it. Now I limped over and let myself in, summoning the bot. It had a queer gait, a half-falling roll that was like a controlled stagger. It clucked over my ribs, applied a salve, waited for the numbness to set it, then taped me up, getting my ribs into alignment.

I stood up, numb from chin to hip, and dismissed the robutler. Its blank face bowed to me as it slid back into its receptacle. Dad let me stay in the hotel room on my birthday sometimes. As I left it, I realized that I'd never see it again.

In the middle of the field, the tethered zepp strained at its mooring lines. The *Spirit of the People's Will* was a Chinese mini-freighter, the kind of thing you could still find in the sky, but Dad collected it anyway. The first time he saw its stubby lines, playful like a kid's toy, he rushed out and got one for the museum. "An instant classic," he called it, "like the Mac, or the Mini. Perfection."

The zepp's cargo hoist was already loaded. Dad must have done that, before getting in the harrier and setting out to defend our turf. The hoist was groaning under a prodigious weight, and I groaned too, once I saw what it was. Dad had put the Carousel onto the hoist.

The Carousel of Progress debuted in 1964, at the New York World's Fair. Walt Disney built it for General Electric—a six-scene robotic stage-play about the role of technology in making our lives better. It was Dad's most treasured possession in the entire world. I seriously believe that if it was a choice between me and it, he might pick it.

In fact, he had sort of done that.

Ten minutes had gone by since I'd made it home, and the sounds of the air battle still raged outside. The zepp was going to have a hard time attaining lift-off with all that weight, and I still hadn't grabbed my own stuff.

Yes, Dad had said to go right away, no delay. Yes, there was a war raging outside the walls. But I wasn't going to leave my friends behind.

The pack's den was in the back of my room, four overgrown canisters that I kept under my desk. The canisters were standard issue brain-storage—drop as much of the nervous system as you can scrape together into one, and it would grow silicon into the ganglia until it had an interface, keeping the whole thing awash in nutrients and wicking waste products out to an evaporator. I had to remember to add a little sugar every now and again, and to whisk away the residue in the evaporator, but apart from that, they did their thing all on their lonesome. Dad had been worried that I wouldn't be able to take care of a pet, let alone four pets, but the pack were the happiest doggies in the state. I'd find them somewhere to live when I got to wherever I was going. I certainly wasn't going to leave them behind.

The Carousel stood so high on the cargo hoist that I was able to simply climb its service ladder to the roof and then reach up and catch the boarding ramp for the gondola. I yanked it down, hearing—but no longer feeling—the pain in my ribs.

The zepp had already warm-booted, all systems nominal. The radars reported a clear liftoff path through Comerica's retracted dome—Dad had added it early on, before I was born, with Mom's help. I had flown the zepp before, but always with Dad at my elbow. It wasn't rocket science, of course. The thing rose until you told it to stop, then moved in whichever direction you steered it. It was a zepp—easier to pilot than a mecha.

The zepp lumbered into the sky, dragged down by the Carousel. We cleared the lip of Comerica and picked up speed, rising a little more cleanly as the Carousel and the zepp made their peace with each other. The lights on the pack's cylinders blinked nervously. I looked around the gondola's open windows, trying to spot the harrier and the battle-platform, half not wanting to see in case what I saw was Dad being blasted out of the sky.

But there they were, Dad still flying circles around the giant thing, its many rotors and gasbags all straining to keep it aloft and stationary. Smaller drones and even a couple of manned planes took off after Dad as I watched and he blasted them out of the sky with contemptuous ease. Dad liked to practice in sims a lot. He might have been the world's greatest organic fighter pilot at this point. Not that that meant much—who cared about being a fighter pilot anymore?

The platform's big guns followed Dad through the sky, seemingly always a little behind him. He anticipated their curve, dodging the twisting, seeking fingers of lightning, the hails of ammo, the guided missiles. He was good—I found myself grinning hard and pumping my fist as Dad took out another battery—but I could see that he wasn't good enough. He had to be good a million times. They had to get lucky once. They would.

As I came up level with the platform, it seemed to notice me, turning a battery toward me. The shells it lofted at me hung in the sky nearby, then sploded in a deadly hail of millions of microscale daisy-cutters. I yanked hard at the yoke and floored it, and the zepp turned away, but not enough. I heard a scritching noise as the deadly little bots skittered on the zepp's armored balloon and gondola, scrabbling for purchase. They rained down past the gondola's windows, like dandruff being shrugged off the zepp's scalp.

Dad's harrier screamed over to the battery that had attacked me, flipping and rolling as he opened up on it, pouring fire down until the side of the platform nearest me literally began to melt, liquefying under withering fire and dripping molten metal in rivulets down the side of the platform. I could see men and mechas running to the affected area, moving up replacement guns, firing on Dad, and then the harrier screamed past me. I caught a glimpse of Dad, in his augmented reflex helmet and crash-suit. He seemed to be saluting me, though he went past so fast I couldn't say for sure. I saluted back and engaged the zepp's props, setting a course east.

I put the zepp on autopilot and turned all the sensor arrays up to maximum paranoia and then went back to watch the dogfight between the harrier and the platform from the rear of the gondola.

Something had hit Dad. There was smoke rising from the mid-section of the harrier, just behind the cockpit. Those things could soak up a lot of damage and still keep turning over, but it was clear, even from this distance, that Dad wouldn't last forever. I found some binox in an overhead compartment and watched Dad dodge and weave. I wanted to call him before I got out of range of our towers, but I didn't want to distract him.

It didn't matter. One of the questing, bent fingers of lightning seized the harrier and followed it as it tried to circle away. Smoke poured from the harrier's engines. The lighting stopped and the harrier began a lazy, wobbly glide toward the platform, Dad's last charge, a suicide trajectory. Two missiles lifted off from the platform, arcing for the harrier, and they caught it before it could crash.

My heart thudded in my ears, audible over the growl of the zepp's turbines. I dialed the binox up higher, letting them auto-track, then switching back over to manual because they kept focusing on the damned *shrapnel*, and I want to find Dad.

Maybe I saw him. It looked like a man in a crash-suit, there amid the rolling smoke and the expanding cloud of metal and ceramic. Looked like a man, maybe, for an instant, lost amid the smoke. Maybe he landed on the platform and fought his way free—or was taken prisoner.

Maybe Dad was still immortal.

In any event, I still was.

PART 2: NO PRIVACY AT ALL AROUND THIS PLACE!

THE CULTISTS DIDN'T MIND THAT I keep the Carousel up and running. Twenty years before, I'd set it down before the old administrative building of the college where they had their headquarters, and they'd never once asked me to shut it down.

Oh, sure, they put a wire in my head, did it on the first day. That wasn't optional: if you stayed with the cultists, you needed to have the wire in your head. It was for the good of the colony.

But being immortal has its advantages, besides the obvious ones. My brain just kind of *ate* that wire—denatured it, anyway. It took a couple weeks, so for the first little while, I was just like all the other cultists, a transceiver for human emotion. I remember that period hazily, but it wasn't altogether terrible. Once you were attuned to the emotions of everyone else in town, everything was kind of . . . It's hard to describe. Huge. Mellow. The emotional state of three million people has a certain inertia, and it's hard to shift in one direction or another. It dampens all the extremes. Sometimes you'd get a *little* happy, or a *little* miserable, but never those raging, spectacular blisses and rages.

It was probably good therapy for me, just then. It probably helped me get by without Dad.

But like I say, it only took a couple weeks for the wire to lose its efficacy. I could still feel a little tickle that let me know, more or less, what the groupmind was thinking, but it never loomed up large. And I could get as angry or happy as I wanted and my neighbors never seemed to notice, so I guess I wasn't transmitting much.

Here's what happened as I steamed east, away from Detroit and the ruins of my father's city/museum. It was smooth sailing for the first couple hours, then I started to hear ominous clunks and thuds. I knew it must be the little daisy cutters. Some of them must have found soft spots in the bag's armor. That was the point of a billion little daisy cutters instead of just one big one—a brute-force attack on the entire defensive perimeter of the target. An attacker only has to find one hole—a defender needs to be seamless.

The zepp's idiot lights got redder and redder as time went by, one critical system after another failing. By the time I thought to bring her down—I was in shock, I guess, plus I was young then—it was too late. Altitude controls were locked.

I watched, helpless, clutching the pack's canisters, as we drifted in the winds, sometimes going higher, sometimes dipping down. The Carousel was a destabilizing force: every time the wind gusted, it rocked like a pendulum, and as the zepp's gyros wound down, we rocked with it.

The zepp set itself down in North Carolina, amid the leftovers of the old UNC campus, settling gently. I slid/stumbled down the ramp with the pack in hand. The zepp was still losing altitude, inching lower and lower. Soon enough, the gondola would come down on the top of the Carousel, doing who-knew-what damage. I did a little executive planning and decided that I had a way better chance of bringing the Carousel up to nominal than I did the daisy-cutter wormed zepp, and I blew the cargo hoist loose, cutting the zepp free so that it lofted away, to ply its idiot way through the skies, unmanned and dying.

∘ ∘ ∘

The thing about immortality is, it's complicated. A mixed blessing. Dad's immortality was a much simpler thing, really: a collection of hacks and tricks to wind back his body's clock, to repair the damage of the ages, to make him young again. Like his yogurt, for his liver.

With me, it was all about the germ plasm. I'd been modded down in my nuclei, a transhuman by birth, a native of the transhuman condition. And no one knew what that meant, really. Including me.

So while it was apparent early on that I was aging slowly—retaining maximal brain plasticity by keeping my physical age as young as possible—no one seemed to suspect just how slowly I was going to age. I was chronologically thirteen when I landed in North Carolina, but I was physically more like ten. At the time, I assumed that meant that I'd just go on, aging slowly, but aging.

Not so, as it turned out.

Twenty years later, I was still eleven. Maybe thirteen. Let me put it this way: no pubes. This was not what I had in mind when I pictured immortality. I had . . . stirrings. But they were like phantom limbs—there but not there, elusive, an itch I couldn't scratch.

The cultists were mildly curious about this, in the same way that they were mildly curious about most things. They weren't worked up about it or anything. They didn't get worked up about anything. That was the point. But they liked having kids and they wanted to know when I'd be ready to help out in that department. So they asked, every now and again, frankly. And I told them the truth. Why not? They weren't going to throw me out—not as long as they thought I was a wirehead.

The only person who had a problem with my perpetual adolescence was me. There were moods that came on me, now and again, sudden and ferocious. Terrors, too. It came with the brain plasticity—I could adapt to anything, but nothing ever stuck. I could never approximate the incredible conviction of the cultists—not even the lesser conviction of the normals who traded with them every now and again. I'd believe something for a day or two—like wanting to overthrow the cult and rescue the wireheads from their surgical bondage—and then it would seem like a stupid idea, and then a distant memory. Only my journals showed me how changeable my weather was. When I got them down off the seat I kept them on in the Carousel and thumbed through them, it wrenched something in my chest. Sometimes I cried. Sometimes I cried for a long time.

Mostly I tried to distract myself from all of this. One good way to do that was to keep the Carousel tuned up. The cultists liked it—it was a relaxing place to sit and watch a show, something they didn't get much of in Raleigh Durham since the wires went in.

The Carousel was a four-part show with a prologue and epilogue, "the longest-running stage show in the history of the world," in which primitive robots told the story of how General Electric and Thomas Edison had rescued them from the dark ages. The robots rotated in and out, appearing behind scrims and delivering corny jokes, singing and tapping their toes, while their electrical appliances clattered, clanked, and showed themselves off.

Dad had loved the Carousel. Not in the "I love chocolate" sense of love. In the "I love you, darling, and I want to marry you and spend the rest of my life with you" sense. Disney World, where the Carousel ended up some time after the '64 World's Fair, had not fared well in the Mecha Wars. All of the Animal Kingdom and Epcot were fused-glass ruins, and most of the Magic Kingdom had burned down. But the Carousel had been only a little scuffed, its control systems fused from EMP weapons.

Dad and I spent a week separating the Carousel from its foundations. It was like digging an old tree out of a forest—digging a wide circle around it, taking the whole root ball with it. In the Carousel's case, it was the control apparatus for the show, spanning two basement levels beneath it. The entire Magic Kingdom was built two stories off the ground, specifically to leave room for the control systems. Over the years, these systems had sprawled sideways and downward, retrofitted solid-state controllers replacing the original mechanicals. We took lots of pictures—visual and millimeter-wave radar—of the whole setup and e-mailed them to a little cluster Dad had that could evolve itself to solve complex vision problems. Overnight, they mailed us back clean architectural as-built diagrams that helped a lot.

Dad had a lot of older, less collectable mechas he kept around for duty like this. We'd driven down to Florida on the path of the old I-75 in a platoon of these things, each of us driving at the head of a column of lumbering beasts that were slaved to our control units. They weren't much to look at, they weren't all that smart, but those big boys were *strong*. Twenty-two of them lifted and carried the Carousel all the way home to Detroit. The pack were in a frenzy once we got back, delighted to have me around again. They'd patrolled the museum-city while we were away, e-mailing me with anything urgent that they didn't know how to cope with. That was before the wumpuses, so there wasn't much by way of risk to our humble home.

Once we got the Carousel home, we set to work restoring it. Dad was insistent that we not fix it *too* well. In a couple of the scenes, the Dad robot was really weird around the neck, its cervical controllers bulging at the flesh like it had swallowed a wheel-rim, sideways. I was pretty sure we could do better than that, but Dad insisted that that was part of the charm, and so I printed a new controller that was an exact match. I even resisted the temptation to replace the glassy, weird eyeballs with something vat-grown from one of my kits.

"It's not supposed to be realistic, Jimmy," he said. "You need to understand that."

I didn't understand it at the time, but I came to understand it eventually. It was the show. It had a dream-like quality, a kind of ethereal logic that seemed perfectly sensible in the show, but which evaporated when the show ended, like the secret technique for levitating evaporating as you wake from sleep.

Each of the four sequences showed the progress that technology made, generation to generation. A wood stove turns into an electric range, then a self-cleaning range, then a voice-controlled microwave oven. At every turn, the world *progressed*, got *better*. The problems posed by each stove got solved. We had lots of different sound-tracks we could run for the ride—it had been redesigned several times—but the original one held the key for me: "At every turn in our history there was always someone saying, 'Turn back. Turn back.' But there is no turning back. Not for us. Not for our carousel. The challenge always lies ahead. And as long as man dreams and works and builds together, these years too can be the best time of your life."

I lived in the future that they were talking about in the ride, but we didn't have "progress" anymore. We'd outgrown progress. What we had was *change*. Things changed whenever anyone wanted to change them: design and launch a fleet of wumpuses, or figure out a way to put an emotional antenna in your head, or create a fleet of killer robots, or invent immortality, or gengineer your goats to give silk. Just do it. It'll catch on, or it won't. Maybe it'll catch itself on. Then the world is . . . different. Then someone else changes it.

The status quo doesn't protect itself; it needs defending if it's going to stay put. The problem is that technology gives more of an advantage to an attacker than to a defender. A defender needs to mount a perfect defense. An attacker needs to find one hole in the defense. So once technology gets going, anything can be knocked down—evil doesn't stand—but nothing much can be erected in its place. Look at Dad's museum.

I've thought about leaving North Carolina and heading back to Detroit, believe me I have. But the cult isn't so bad. They're all nice and friendly and they come as close to stability as anything I've ever experienced. Plus they're pretty good with medical technology, and their biologists don't mind if I ask them nosy, ignorant questions about curing my immortality—at least enough to get my testicles to descend.

Twenty years have gone by and I have two—count 'em, two—pubic hairs. I call them Yeti and Sasquatch. I am as flexible as a ten-year-old—I can get my forehead down on my knee or clasp my arms over my shoulder—and I can run around all day. But like I said, I can't stay interested in much for longer than a few days. My brain and body are so plastic that I can't manage to do anything that requires any kind of stability. I'm like the perfect metaphor for the whole world.

No one knows how to deimmortalize me yet. All I want is a little bit of it, a little bit of aging. A couple more years. Life's pretty good at eighteen, it seems to me. Eighteen would be a good age.

o o o

I didn't recognize Lacey when I saw her. It had been twenty years, and the years had changed her.

I was out in the bush, looking for wild mushrooms. Mostly you got kombucha, big ones, and they made delicious tea. Supposedly they were a little hallucinogenic, but it appeared that my marvelous immortal liver didn't much care to have me enter a state of elevated reality, so all I got out of it was tea. It was good tea, though.

I had the pack with me. I'd built them new bodies, better suited to the quiet life among the cultists. The bodies resembled furry mechanical squirrels. They could crawl all over you without freaking you out or making you feel threatened, which was exactly what I wanted from them. They were still frisky, even though they had aged a little and become a little less experimental, a little more prone to hanging around the Carousel and its immediate grounds. The canisters containing their nervous systems and brains could keep them alive for some time yet, I was sure, but they wouldn't live forever. Lucky little bastards.

It was crisp autumn and the leaves were ten million flaming colors, crunching underfoot as we sought out the kombuchas. I was bending to inspect something that Pepe had found—Pepe still loved to have more than one PoV, so I'd given him four squirrels to drive at once—and when I looked up, I was staring into her boots, lace-up numbers, old fashioned with thick waffle-soles.

I kept looking up. She was a woman, in her mid-thirties. Her hair had grown out into an irregular mob of curls, her round face rosy-cheeked from the chilly weather. Fine lines radiated out from her drawn-up bow lips, and her eyes had small lines to match at their corners.

"Hello," I said. She wasn't a wirehead, I could tell that just by looking at the hair. They liked to wear it short so as not to interfere with the antenna.

"Jimmy?" she said, putting her hand to her chest. She was wearing a smart cowl that breathed gently around her, keeping her warm and dry.

I cocked my head, trying to place her. She looked so familiar, but I couldn't place her, not exactly—

"Jimmy!" she said, and grabbed me in a hard hug. There was a woman under that cowl, boobs and hips. She was a whole head taller than me. But the smell was the same. Or maybe it was the hug.

"Lacey!" I said, and squeezed back, barely getting my arms around her.

She practically lifted me off my feet, and she squeezed so hard that all the breath went out of me.

"Lacey!" I croaked, "easy there!"

She set me down, a little reluctantly, and took a step back. "Jesus Christ, Jimmy, you haven't changed *at all*."

I shrugged. "Immortal," I said.

She put her hand to her chest and looked at me, her mouth open. "Yeah, of course," she said. "Immortal."

"I'm trying to cure it," I said. "Not all the way. But I thought if I could age up to, you know, eighteen or so . . ."

"Jimmy," she said, "please stop talking about this for now. I'm out of weirdness quotient for the day."

I had some snacks in my bag—the tortillas and tomatoes that the cult favored for staple crops—so I sat down and spread out my picnic tarp and offered her a seat, then something to eat.

She sat down and we ate together. We used to do this, back in Detroit, sneak picnics together out in the boonies, in an abandoned building or, in a pinch, cupped in one of my mecha's hands. We fell into the easy rhythm of it as though no time at all had passed since then. For me, none had—at least not physically.

I told her about the zepp ride and the daisy cutters, about the slow landing and my settling in here, bound to the Carousel, not wanting to abandon it.

She got a little misty when she remembered the attack on Detroit. "I remember the zeppelin lifting off, and all the explosions in the sky. I was hiding under something—a truck, I think—and trying to keep the goat from going crazy. What was her name? Louisa?"

"Moldavia," I said. I couldn't believe she didn't remember that. It was like yesterday to me.

"Moldavia! We ate her, you know. I remember that now. Mom and Dad couldn't get their silk into India and the farm took a turn for the worse and—"

She broke off and rolled up another chopped tomato salad in another tortilla, sprinkled some basil and cilantro on it from the little herb bag I kept.

"What happened afterward?" I asked. "What happened to Detroit?"

"Oh," she said. "Oh, well. The wumpuses came, of course. Took about two weeks for them to get through it all, and when they were done, there were so many of them that they mostly ate each other for another week, which was really gross, but when that was done, there was just good land. We farmed it for a while. Mostly redwoods. Big ones—four-hundred-footers. Anything for a carbon-credit. They were cheap and easy."

I closed my eyes and rocked back on my tailbone. I'd stood by the Carousel for twenty years because, somewhere in my mind, I expected that Dad would be getting the museum back together and that wherever the Carousel was, he would come. He wouldn't abandon it.

Somewhere in the back of my mind, I expected that Dad was alive, immortal, coming for me. That we'd have our immortality together. It was lonely, being the only one.

"Redwoods," I finally said. It came out in a croak.

"Big mutant ones," she said, eating her burrito, apparently oblivious to me. "Didn't last, of course. What does? They all got some kind of blight that petrified them where they stood. We think it was some kind of exotic mesoite that traded their carbon for calcium, harvesting the good stuff for who-knows-what. It went top down, so it took a while for us to notice. For a while, they all stayed upright, white and chalky. Then they crumbled until they were nothing but powder, which blew away."

"What doesn't?" I said. I was still thinking of Dad. I knew I'd get over it, though. Brain plasticity.

"Yeah," she said. "Mom and Dad hung in there with the rest of the Treehuggers for a while, but I wasn't going to stay there forever, I knew that much. I went west on my sixteenth, got as far as the Oregon coast. Kept in touch with the parents for a while, but they moved to Bangalore when I was about twenty-five and so that was it for them and me. I dated this guy who found me a job maintaining these weird brain-scanners at a research facility and I did that for a while too, which would have given my parents seizures if they knew. I probably stayed in that job for longer than I would have, just for that reason.

"But the people who ran the research station got bored or went broke—they didn't ever tell us peons—and one day they didn't show up for work. We all kept coming in and cleaning the floors and keeping the machines running and signing for deliveries for a week, but then we figured that they weren't coming back. So I hit the road again (the boyfriend didn't last as long as the job) and now I'm here. And so are you!"

She ate another burrito. She could really put them away.

She told me more minutiae from the road, places she'd been and people she'd met, talking for a long, long time. So long that I started to shiver as the sun dipped low. The pack whined around me, climbing up on my lap and my shoulders and head. Lacey was oblivious to the passage of time, her cowl keeping her warm. I had one like it that I'd bought from a traveler a couple years before, but I didn't wear it much—it was too big for me and it tripped me up a little.

"We got to get going," I said. "I'm freezing."

She stopped talking and looked around. There was something hunted in her look. She stood up and slapped at her cowl to knock the crumbs off it and then she looked around again.

"So," she said. "So. Nice to see you again, Jimmy. Really nice! You can send me e-mail or something sometime if you want to. Good luck with everything."

I stopped folding up the tarp and putting away the leftovers. "Why? Where are you going?"

She looked around for a third time, then pointed south. "That direction looks promising. Do you know what's there?"

I followed her finger through the woods. "About half a day's walk will get you down to Jordan Lake. Nice places around there. Holiday cottages. Keep on going and you'll hit Myrtle Beach, eventually. Might take you a week or two. Where are you headed, anyway?"

"It was really great to see you." She grabbed me in another one of those hugs, so fierce that I couldn't breathe for a moment.

"Where are you going?" I said again, once she'd released me.

She felt in her cowl and found a hanky, blew her face on it and wiped away all the stuff she'd started leaking all of a sudden.

"I just go," she said, finally. "That's all I've done for the past two years, Jimmy. I just go, and keep going. All the places are different, but they're all the same, too. Nothing's like what I'm looking for."

"What are you looking for?"

"I don't know, but I'll know it when I see it. I just hope that I find it soon."

"If you go off that way, you're going to end up walking all night before you get to a hotel."

She laughed. "I don't really . . . use . . . hotels," she said. "I stay out here, with all the nature. Product of my upbringing. Once a Treehugger . . ."

I hadn't had a real conversation in ten years. It was a million-to-one chance, running into Lacey in the woods. Also: maybe she knew a little more about Detroit?

"Why don't you come over to my place?" I said at last. "I've got plenty of room. I promise you, my place isn't the same."

She crouched down and looked in my eyes. "I don't think that's such a good idea, Jimmy," she said. "But thank you."

We didn't really argue. We hardly discussed it. But somehow, she ended up taking my hand and letting me lead her back home, ducking the occasional wirehead on the way.

Back in Detroit, my dad had reconstructed the Carousel's elaborate concrete ramp and queue area, but I didn't have the resources to do that here, so to get up on my Carousel's apron, you had to scramble up a chest-high wall that shielded the machinery beneath the stage and seats. I got myself up—the pack skittered up around me, scaling the wall as though it were horizontal—and then I helped Lacey up. Her hands were strong and her palms were dry, her fingertips calloused and raspy on my wrists.

"This way," I said, and led her inside.

Of course, I wasn't running the show at the time. I don't, usually. Not that I have power woes—the cell that Dad fitted it with won't run out of isotopes for a couple centuries yet, but it saves wear-and-tear on the parts, and those can be a bitch to replace.

The Carousel is designed to seat six audiences at once, rotating continuously around the stage in 60-degree wedges. Between each stage is a little baffle that soaks up the noise from the adjoining set and provides a little space for the operators to hide out from the customers. At least, that's how I used it. I suppose I could have set my bed up on one of the stages, or on the sloping auditorium aisles. I could have even removed some of the painstakingly restored seats. But all that felt wrong, after all the work that Dad put into getting it all so cherry and pristine.

So I kept my bedroll in the gap between the first two scenes, and my clothes and things between the remaining gaps. The pack's canisters were stashed under the stage in the third scene, which held a little maintenance hollow where we'd always kept tools and such.

Lacey laughed when I let her in. "You live here?"

"I forget, did you ever get to ride this?"

"No, but I remember when you brought it back. We all came out to watch the mechas carry it through our forest. You knocked down a bunch of trees to make way."

I shrugged. "It's a wide load."

"So what's it do?"

I showed her, turning it on and then rushing to sit down next to her. The lights went down and the curtains parted, and a spotlight played over the old "General Electric" logo. I loved that logo. Imagine a time when there were companies that made their fortune being generally electrical! These days, electrical stuff was very specific indeed.

The narration started. Dad told me that the actor's name was Jean Shepherd, and I'd heard his spiel a billion times, so often that I sometimes mixed up his calm, warm baritone with my memory of my father's voice, the two all blended in my infinitely plastic mind. The narrator welcomed us to Walt Disney's Carousel of Progress and told us some of its history, then started with the real heavy philosophy: "The challenge always lies ahead. And as long as man dreams and works and builds together, these years too can be the best time of your life."

I looked at Lacey to see if she'd noticed the way that the voice-over had just dropped that on us. The challenge always lies ahead. Progress! She was looking heavy-lidded, but attentive.

The curtains parted and we got to the first scene. Dad—not my dad, the dad on stage—was wearing a cravat and fanning himself with a newspaper. The dog lay at his feet, doing comedy barks. Dad told us all about the miracle of his ice-box ("holds fifty pounds of ice!") and his gas lamps. Then the lights came up on the scrim scenes on the wings of the stage and we got to meet Mom, who was ironing. Mom complained that even though it only takes five hours to do the laundry with her new "wash-day marvel," her spare time is taken up with canning and cleaning the oven. This is supposed to be funny.

Then the other side lit up and we got to meet Jimmy. Not me—the son. His name is also Jimmy. I'm sure it's just a coincidence. After all, I'd been around for years before Dad got the Carousel. And Mom probably wouldn't have let him name me after an old robot. Probably.

Jimmy was looking through a stereoscope at pornography—well, pictures of hoochie-coochie girls—and Dad gave him a good-natured ribbing. I'd seen this scene hundreds of times, but this time, sitting next to Lacey, remembering our necking sessions, it made me a little uncomfortable.

The remaining scenes introduced Sister (in a corset, worrying that she is "indecent") and Grandma and Grandpa, listening to a "talking machine" with their pet parrot.

Then it was over and the singing started, "There's a great big beautiful tomorrow/Shining at the end of every day!" and the stage rotated. We came around to the next scene—the 1920s and electricity—and I heard a sound from Lacey, beside me. She was snoring. Her head was down on her chest and she was sleeping soundly. Her lips were parted a little and her face looked worried in sleep. I realized that she'd looked worried since I'd met her.

I got up and stopped the ride, resetting all the shows and powering them down. From the six slices of the Carousel, I heard the robots ceasing their spiels and going to sleep. The pack—who didn't much care for the show—came out of hiding and began to race around the aisles, nipping at each others' heels.

Lacey was going to have to sleep somewhere. I hadn't really thought about that. I went and checked out my narrow bed. I'd filled the space between two stages with a pile of pillows. It was comfortable enough. Did it smell bad? Maybe it did. The shower was outside, in a little prefab building I'd bought off a traveler, and I didn't always remember to use it.

Lacey probably had some kind of bed, anyway. I got up and grabbed her pack. It felt like it was full of rocks. Man, she had to be *strong*. Another perk of adulthood—of mortality.

I gave her shoulder a little shake, and her head lolled and she snored. I gave her another shake, a little harder this time. Her eyes opened a crack, then she straightened up slowly and opened and closed her mouth a few times.

"It's been a long day," she said. "Sorry, Jimmy."

I showed her my bed and she laughed. "It's like the den of some burrowing animal."

I felt obscurely ashamed. Twenty years here and I had practically nothing to show for it. The pack's new bodies. The maintenance I'd done on the Carousel. My pathetic pile of pillows.

She put her arm around my shoulders and gave me a squeeze. "It's great," she said. "It's just the kind of thing I would have loved, twenty years ago." That made me feel even worse. I slumped.

"Poor Jimmy," she said. "You're very generous to offer me a place to sleep, you know."

"Do you have a bed in your pack?"

She nodded. "I do, indeed. But screw it. It's a pain to set up. I don't need it here. Besides, I'm so tired I could drop where I stand. Where's the bathroom?"

I told her, warning her to keep a low profile—I wasn't sure how I was going to explain her to the cultists, who'd want her to get a wire in her head if she wasn't just passing through—and started to dig through my clothes, looking for enough stuff to make another bed out of between two of the other theater-sections.

She came back, shivering a little, clapping her hands together. "Cold around here at night," she said, before casually pulling her cowl over her head, then stripping off her sweater—spidergoat silk, it looked like—and then her tights. Just as quick as that, she was naked.

I'd never seen a naked woman before. I know that sounds silly, but physiologically, I was still a little kid. I didn't have a girlfriend. Every now and again, I'd get a little curious about it, feel something that might be horniness, like an itch somewhere in my lower belly, but most of the time I didn't think about sex. The cultists had plenty of sex, but behind closed doors. Once I'd seen some pornography that a traveler had brought through, but she'd snatched it away as soon as she noticed me eyeballing it, warning me that this wasn't the kind of thing a kid like me should be looking at. I didn't bother to explain my unique chronological circumstances.

My eyes were flicking from one part of her to another. Her breasts. Her thighs. The curls at her pubis. I'd seen Dad naked every now and again, but not for decades. I'd seen pubic hair before, but it had never been this interesting. She had little tufts of hair in her armpits, too. So much hair!

She seemed not to notice me staring, but she eventually turned away and bent to rummage in her pack. Her genitals winked at me as she did. I realized that I had an erection, a strange little boner in my pants. I got them now and again, and they were usually just a nuisance, something that got in the way.

She straightened up, holding a long shirt that she slipped into. It hung down to her thighs.

"All right," she said. "Me to bed. You sleep left or right?"

It took me a minute to get that she was asking me a question. I blinked a couple times. "What?"

"Left or right side of the bed? I can do either."

I fumbled for words. "I'm going to sleep over there." I pointed at the pile of clothes I'd been assembling.

She clucked her tongue and crossed her eyes. "Don't be stupid. There's room for both of us there. I'm not going to put you out of your bed. Get in."

I hesitated.

"Get in!" she said, clapping her hands.

I turned away and awkwardly stripped down to my underpants and shirt. I worried again that I might smell. I didn't wash my clothes all that often. They were wicking and dirt-shedding and had impregnated antibacterials, so I didn't see why I should. But maybe I smelled. The cultists wouldn't say anything. Wireheads didn't notice that kind of thing.

She clapped her hands again and pointed at the pillow. "March, young man!"

Then I was whirling back in time. That was what Dad used to say when I was dragging my ass around. Had I told her that? Did she know it anyway? Had she guessed? Was it a coincidence?

She repeated herself and pointed. I crawled into the bed. The pack bounded in after me, assuming their usual positions all around me, snuggling and burrowing among the pillows. She laughed.

A moment later, the pillows shifted around me as she climbed in next to me. I tried to press myself up against my wall, giving her as much space as possible, but she gathered me in her arms and squeezed me like a teddy bear.

"Good night, Jimmy," she said. Her face smelled of soap and her hair smelled of woodsmoke. It tickled my cheeks. She kissed the top of my head.

A weird thing happened then. I stopped thinking about her being naked. I stopped thinking about her being my old friend Lacey. Suddenly, all I could think about was how good this felt, being held to a soft bosom, enfolded in strong arms. Dad hugged me plenty. But I didn't remember my mother. She'd died not long after I was born. Poisoned by Detroit. She hadn't eaten her yogurt, didn't get her microbes, and so her liver gave out. Dad barely talked about her, and the photos of her had vanished with Detroit itself, consumed by some wumpus and turned into arable land.

Lacey squeezed me again, and I found that I was crying. Silently at first, then I must have let out a whimper because she went, "Shhh, shhh," and squeezed me harder. "It's OK," she murmured into my hair, and words like that, and rocked me back and forth, and then I was crying harder.

I cried myself out there in the pillows, in Lacey's arms. I don't know what I wept for, but I remember the feeling as not altogether sad. There was some joy there, a feeling of homecoming in the arms of my old friend. The pack snuggled in among us, and they were ticklish, so soon we were both laughing and rocking back and forth.

"Good night, Lacey," I said.

"Good night, Jimmy," she said. She kissed the top of my head again and squeezed me harder and I let myself relax in her arms.

o o o

The wireheads don't mind the occasional houseguest, but anyone who's going to actually *live* in the settlement needs to join the cult. They don't want any violent, emotional, unpredictable people running around, making things difficult for them. The deal is a simple one: get the wire in your head, get free food, shelter, and community forever. Don't get the wire in your head and you have to get out of town.

You'd be surprised at how many people don't want to play along with this system (I guess I count as one of those people). The cult's gotten pretty good at spotting freeloaders who want to live in the peace and prosperity of the cult but don't want to join up. These people seem to think that so long as they're doing their share of the work, they should be able to stick around. What they don't understand is that the work isn't the important part: robots can do the heavy lifting, as much as we let them do of it.

The important thing is the stability. Here in wirehead country, nothing important ever changes. New people come in. Old people die. Babies are born. Kids go to school—I went with them for a little while, in my wirehead days, but I decided I didn't need to keep going to classes after three or four years, and no one seemed to mind. No one minds what anyone else does, once you're a wirehead. Since we can all feel each others' emotions, it's impossible to resent someone without him knowing about it, and it's impossible to feel guilty without letting others know it. Your whole attitude toward your neighbors is on permanent display, visible from a mile off. My own antenna seems to radiate a calm acceptance no matter what I'm feeling, and lets me know what others are feeling without swamping me with their emotions.

The work gets done. "Progress" never happens. We've banished progress, here in the wirehead cult. That's OK by me, I suppose. Who needs it?

"So I had been living in Florida, up near Jacksonville, in wiki country," Lacey said, over our breakfast. I kept a larder of fresh fruit in the maintenance space under the stage, and Lacey had been glad to help me slice up a couple of delicious fruit salads. I'd put up some yogurt a few days before and it was mature enough to pour overtop, with some sunflower seeds left over from the last autumn. "The city was good, but it got to me, all that change, all the time. I tried to garden a little patch of it, just a little spot where I could put up a house, but there were so many trolls who kept overwriting my planning permission with this idea for a motorcycle racing track. I'd revert their changes, they'd revert back. Then one of the Old Ones would come by and freeze my spot for a month and lecture us. Then they'd be back at Day 31. I only met them face to face once. I'd pictured them as old Florida bikers, leathery and worn, but they were teenagers! Just kids."

I looked away, at the blue sky overhead, visible through the riotous colors of the leaves.

"Sorry," she said. "You know what I mean, though. They were like, eight sixteen-year-olds, and they'd built their bikes to burn actual hydrocarbons. These things made so much goddamned noise! Your old mecha was quieter! They rode them up to my house one day, left all six in my garden, among my flowers, growling, and rang my doorbell.

"I had built a little gypsy caravan with flower-boxes and bright paint, all prefab vat-grown woodite, impervious to weather and bugs, watertight at the seams, breathing through a semipermeable roof and floor. It was a really nice piece of engineering—my parents would have liked it!

"I answered the door and they pointed to their motorcycles and explained that they'd spent an entire year building and tuning them and that my little house was the only thing stopping them from building a racetrack. They wanted me to move the house to somewhere else. They were extra pissed because my house had *wheels*, so how hard could it be to relocate? They even offered to find me somewhere else, get me a tow. I told them no, I liked it there, liked my garden (what was left of it), liked the creek down the hill from me, liked my view of the big city down the other side of the hill, all its lights.

"They told me that their parents had lots of money and they could get me a real big place somewhere up high in the city, maybe even put my caravan on a roof there." She stopped talking while we picked our way down a hillside. We were headed for my own creek, which was cold and brisk, but still swimmable, for a week or two. I'd brought a bar of soap.

"I told them to get off my land. I also recorded them from my front window as they shouted things at me and threw stuff at my door. It turned out to be dead animals. They left a dead rabbit or squirrel on my doormat every day for a week. I added pictures to the Discuss page for the zoning, and the Old Ones were properly affronted and froze their editing privileges.

"But they didn't let up. They had a whole army of sock-puppets they were paying in Missouri, a boiler-room outfit where they'd do actual work on the wiki, improve it a lot, build up credibility and make themselves very welcome, then come and edit my zoning. It got so I was doing nothing but staying home all day and reverting and arguing with these guys.

"Then I went away for a couple days—there was a bar-becue festival in a big field outside of town and I got invited to compete, so I was working over a smoker there, and when I got back, guess what?"

"Your caravan was gone and they were racing motor-cycles where it used to be."

"Exactly," she said. "Exactly. They'd knocked down the trees, dammed the stream, paved everything, put in half-pipes. Even if I changed the zoning back, I wouldn't want to live there again."

"I woulda been pissed," I said, getting down to my skin and jumping into the stream, sputtering and blowing. Normally I'd have waded in a few millimeters at a time, but I was still uncomfortable being nude in front of her, so I just plunged. She followed suit.

"You'd think, huh?" she said. "But I was just resigned at that point. I moved to the city, which had its own charms. Remember that they said they could get me a rooftop? Well, it turns out that roofs were easy to get. Not many people want to sleep on the ninetieth floor of a tower, but I found it as peaceful as anything. I strung up my hammock and put up my tents and settled in to love my view."

Sometimes it was hard to remember that this was *Lacey Treehugger*, the girl who'd thought that all concrete was a sin. Ninety floors up! Damn.

There were more people coming down to the creek. Double damn. Lacey had been there three days and we had managed to avoid my neighbors the whole time, but my luck had run out.

They had the typical wirehead look: one-piece, short-sleeved garments that shed dirt, so they glowed faintly. Stripes and piping were the main decoration. Someone had designed this outfit in the early days of the cult and no one had ever re-designed it. Of course not. Why change anything around here?

There were three of them. I recognized them at once: Sebastien, a guy in his twenties whom I'd known since he was a baby; Tina, an older woman with teak-colored skin; and Brent, her son, who was eleven, the same as me, sort of.

"Hello there," Sebastien said. I felt the tickle of their emotions from the vestiges of my antenna, a kind of oatmeal-bland wash of calm nullity. "Haven't seen you in a few days." He noticed Lacey and squinted at her. She had sunk down so that only her round face stuck up out of the sluggish water. "Hello to you, too," he said. "I'm Sebastien, this is Tina and Brent." They all waved, except for Brent, who was bending down and examining a frog he'd found on a flat rock.

"This is my friend Lacey," I said. Sebastien drove me crazy. He was born and bred to the cult and always wanted to talk to me about how much better life was now that I was living with the wireheads. He was the kind of zealot who made me worry that if I didn't match his enthusiasm that he'd try to figure out if my antenna was working properly. Talking to him always put me on my guard.

Lacey waved.

"We're here for a swim," he said, like it wasn't obvious. He didn't ask if we minded—no wirehead would—but instead just started stripping down to the bathing trunks he wore under his jumpsuit, giving me an accidental glimpse of his bony ass. Tina did the same, taking his hand and squeezing it, then Brent struggled out of his. Tina and her ex-husband had Brent and then split when he was still a baby, one of those weird, calm wirehead divorces, so mellow they might as well be happening underwater.

They slipped into the water with us and I knew I was going to have to say something. "I'm sorry," I said, "but we're not wearing anything in here. Do you mind looking away while we get out?"

Sebastien and Tina had made it in to their shins, their bodies broken out in gooseflesh from the icy, bracing water. "Oh, Jimmy," Tina said. "We're sorry." All three of them caught her sadness and looked downcast. Reflexively, I looked sad too. Gradually, they caught the larger emotion of the group, still perceptible at this distance, and got happier again.

"Don't worry about it," I said once the sun had risen on their moods again. "It was inconsiderate of us. I didn't think anyone else would be down by the river on a day like this."

"We like it cold," Sebastien said. "Wakes up the body." Then Brent took a few toddling steps into the water, slipped, and splashed them. They laughed and splashed him back. There was a moment of frenzy as they caught each others' surprise and glee, and then it, too, dampened down.

"Well, we're just about done here," I said.

"Nice to meet you," Lacey said. They'd turned their backs, but I caught Brent sneaking a peek before he looked away, too.

"Nice to meet you, too," Tina said. "You be sure and come by the general meeting tonight, all right?"

I grunted as noncommittally as I could, while pulling on my jumpsuit over my wet legs. It wicked away the wet as I struggled into it. I just wanted to get away from there—they were curious about Lacey, I could tell that even without a fully functional antenna.

Lacey just pulled her smartcloak over her head and let her boots conform themselves to her feet. We had walked idly and slowly to the river, but we hurried away.

"I'm not supposed to be here, am I?" Lacey said.

"No," I said. "Yes." I helped her up onto the side-trail that I used when I didn't want to talk to anyone. "It's complicated. They're going to want you to get wired, or leave."

"And getting wired—you wouldn't recommend it?"

I shrugged. "They're nice people. If you had to choose a group of people to share your state of mind with, they'd be a pretty good choice."

"But you don't think it's a good idea."

I shrugged again. "I let them put a wire in my head," I said.

"Your brain ate it, though."

I looked around, suddenly paranoid. There was no one. "Shhh. Yes, but I didn't know that my brain would eat it when I let them install it."

"So why'd you do it?"

I thought back. "I was a kid," I said at last. "I'd just lost my Dad and my home. They were nice to me. They said that they'd leave me alone once I had the wire fitted. That was all I wanted."

"Did you like it?"

"Having a wire? Well, not the worst thing in the world, having a wire. I never felt lonely. And when I was sad, it passed quickly. I think it would have been a lot harder without it."

"So you think it's therapeutic, then? Maybe I should get one after all."

I turned around and took her hands. "Don't, OK? Please. I like you this way."

We got home and sat down in the theater seats. I thought we'd talk about it, but we seemed to have run out of words. I wished for a moment that we had matching antennae so I could know what she was feeling. That was pretty weird.

"Show me this play," she said. "I fell asleep the other night."

So I started it up. I'd done a major, three-year-long maintenance project on it that had just wrapped up, so it was running as good as new. I was proud of the work I'd done. I wished that Dad could see it. Lacey was nearly as good.

We sat through the opening scene, rotated around the arc by 60 degrees, and went through the change to the Roaring Twenties. The family's kitchen was now filled with yarn-like wires coming off the ceiling light and leading to all the appliances. Dad was wearing a bow tie now and fanning himself with Souvenir of Niagara Falls fan. Dad wants to show us all his new modern appliances, so they all switch on and start flapping and clacking while frenetic music plays in the background. Then a "fuse" blows—I looked this up, it means that he overloaded a crude breaker in the power-supply—and the whole street goes dark. A neighbor threatens to beat him, but then "Jimmy"—yes, Jimmy again—changes the fuse and the lights come back.

Mom and Sister are getting into costume—there's a Fourth of July party that night—and Dad has to join them, but he gets us to sing his song. I noted that Lacey tapped her toe as we went around the arc, and it made me feel very good.

o o o

After the show, I made us diner and Lacey told me more funny stories from the road. Then we crawled into bed and she enfolded me in her arms. We'd done that every night. I didn't cry anymore, and it felt so good. Like something I'd always missed.

"They're going to come for you," I said, lying with my eyes open, feeling her arms around me.

"They are, huh?"

"Put a wire in your head."

"And you don't think I should do that."

"I'll go with you." I swallowed. "If you want."

She squeezed me harder. "I don't think you'll be able to carry this thing, do you?"

"I don't mind."

"Liar. You've been taking care of this thing for twenty years, Jimmy!"

"That was when I thought that Dad would come back for it. Doesn't seem like he'll come back now. Stupid terrorists."

"Who?"

"The assholes who attacked Detroit. Whoever they were." I noticed that she'd stiffened a little. "I thought they were thieves at first, after our stuff. But from what you say, it sounds like they were terrorists—they just wanted to destroy it all. We probably had the last mountain of steel-belted radials in the world, you know?"

She didn't say anything for a bit. "I can go in the morning. We can stay in touch."

"I want to go with you." I surprised myself with the vehemence of it. "I need to get away from here. I need to get away from this *thing*." I punched out at the wall at the edge of the bed, giving it a hard thump and sending the pack scurrying around in circles. "Fuck this thing. It's a prison. It's stuck me down here. Just another one of Dad's stupid ideas."

"You shouldn't talk about your Dad that way. He was—"

"What? He was an asshole! Look at me! Do you think I want to be like *this* forever?"

"You told me that you thought you'd found a cure for it—"

I laughed. "Sure, sure. But I've thought that for twenty years. Nothing's worked."

She hugged me tighter. "It's not all bad, is it? It could be worse. You could be getting old, like me. I get what I can out of the neutraceuticals, but you know, it gets harder every day. I can't walk as far as I used to. Can't see as well. Can't hear as well. I'm getting wrinkled, I keep finding grey hairs—"

"Come on," I said. "You're a beautiful woman. You got to grow up. I'm just a little kid! I'm going to stay a little kid forever. You got to change. Not just change, either—*progress*! You got to progress, to get better and smarter and wiser and, you know, *more*!"

"I'm just saying it's not as good as you think it is."

"You get to have sex!" I blurted. "You get to know what it's like."

"You've never?"

"Never," I said. "Physiologically, I'm eleven or twelve. No adult would have sex with me. And it's not right for me to make out with little kids. The last girl I kissed was you, Lacey."

"Oh, Jimmy," she said. She stroked my hair. "I'm sorry. It's hard to know how to think of you. Sometimes I think you're just a little kid, but you're actually a little older than me, aren't you?"

"Yeah," I said. "But my brain doesn't age much either. It's too plastic. I don't get to build up layers of experience one on top of another—it slips out underneath. I really have to concentrate to think properly. The local scientists would be freaked out about this if they could be freaked out about anything. This is probably the only place in the world where never changing is considered to be a signal virtue."

I realized that I was balling up my fists and so I relaxed them and took some deep breaths. Lacey was snuggled up against me and it was warm and good. I tried to focus on that, and not the yawning pit in my gut.

"You're not going to take me with you, are you?"

She swallowed. "We'll see."

I knew what that meant.

I tried not to let her hear me cry, but it shook my ribs, and she hugged me harder. She didn't say, "I'll take you with," though. Of course not. She didn't want to have a kid, an instant son.

o o o

I woke from a strange dream of kissing and sliding skin. I had a rock hard erection, like nothing I'd ever felt before. There was that itch again, in my belly, that I supposed meant "horny," though I'd never felt it like this. Lacey had drooped away from me in her sleep and was lying on her back beside me. In the dim light of the pack's glowing power-indicators, I could see her chest rising and falling, her nipples visible through the thin fabric of her nightshirt. I remembered what she'd looked like naked the other night. She must have noticed my reaction, because she'd changed in private every night since. I realized that that was what I'd been dreaming of.

I reached out with a tentative hand and let it barely graze over her breast. She didn't stir. It felt soft, giving under my finger. My mouth was bone dry. I pulled back the coverlet. Her long t-shirt had ridden up, and I could see her legs all the way up to the curve of her hip. I touched her hip, stroking it with the same hesitancy. Warm. Jouncy—firm but giving. I touched her thigh. She muttered something and stirred.

I froze. She put one hand on her tummy, and her shirt rucked up higher. Now I could see all her hair down there. It was too dark to see anything more. I put my hand on her thigh again, halfway up. Her breathing didn't change. I slid my hand higher. Higher still.

My smallest finger brushed up against something very soft and a little moist, something that felt like a warm mushroom.

"Jimmy?"

I knew that she was awake, fully awake. I snatched my hand away.

"God, I'm sorry Lacey."

"What are you doing, Jimmy?"

"I—" I couldn't find the words. It was too embarrassing, too weird. Too creepy.

"It was the sex talk, huh?"

I swallowed. I calmed myself down. I decided I could talk about this like a man of science. "I'm not quite physiologically there, when it comes to sex. I'm sort of stuck between the first stage of sexual maturity and childhood. Normally, it's not a problem, but . . ." I ran out of science.

"Yeah," she said. "I wondered about that. Come here, Jimmy."

Awkwardly, I snuggled up to her, letting her spoon behind me.

"No," she said. "Turn around."

I turned around. I had my little boner again, and I was conscious of how it must be pressing against her thigh, the way her breasts were pressed against my chest. Her face was inches from mine, her breath warm on my lips.

She kissed me.

She kissed *exactly* like I remembered it, twenty years before. Slowly, with a lazy bit of tongue. Her teeth were warm in her mouth as I tentatively reciprocated. She took my hand and put it on her breast. Her nipple was a little bump in the center of my palm, the flesh of her breast yielding under my hand. I squeezed it and rubbed it and touched it, almost forgetting the kiss. She laughed a little and pulled her shirt up and pulled my face down to her breasts. I kissed them, kissed the nipples, unsure of what to do but hearing her breath catch when I did something right. I tried to do more of that. It was fascinating. The pack roused itself and squirmed over us. I pushed them away.

She gave a soft little moan. Her hands roamed over my back, squeezed my butt. Her hand found my little boner. I gave a jolt, then another as she started to move her hand. Then I felt something like a sneeze, that started in my stomach and went *down*. There was sticky stuff on her hand.

"Wow," I said. "I didn't know I could do that."

"Let's find out what else you can do," she said.

○ ○ ○

The next day was my scheduled day at the research station, but I didn't want to leave Lacey alone in the Carousel, not now that Sebastien and Tina knew about her. They might come by to ask her some questions about her intentions.

Besides, there was the matter of what we'd done the night before. It had lasted for a long time. There was a lot I didn't know. When we were done, I knew a *lot* more. And it was all I could think of, from the moment I woke up with the smells on me and the small aches here and there; while I was in the bathroom and pissing through a dick that felt *different*, gummy and sticky; while I was washing up and digging some grapefruits out of my storehouse for breakfast, slicing them open and grabbing water from the osmotic filter for the day.

Lacey was sitting up in bed, the pack arrayed around her, the sheet not covering her beautiful breasts. Her hair was in great disarray and her mouth was a little puffy and swollen from kissing.

"Good morning," she said, and smiled at me, her little bow mouth widening into a giant grin.

I smiled back and handed her a grapefruit. I cuddled up to her as we ate and she laughed when I got a squirt of grapefruit in the eye. We didn't say much, but then the Flea, who is also in charge of my calendar reminders, began to chitter at me to tell me it was time to go to the lab.

"What's he want?"

"I'm supposed to see the researchers here. About my immortality. I go every couple of weeks and they do more tests, measure me. Whatever Dad did to my germline wasn't documented anywhere public. He had all these buddies around the world who had treated themselves to make them immortal, and they were all refining the process. None of them seem to be anywhere that we can find them, so we're trying to reverse-engineer them."

"What kind of researchers would a place like this have? I'd have thought that they would be pretty hostile to R&D in a place that isn't supposed to change."

"Well, when the whole world is changing all the time, it takes a lot of R&D to respond to it so that you don't change along with it. Some of them are pretty good. I looked up their bios. They were highly respected before they became wireheads. Mellowing out your emotions shouldn't interfere with your science anyway."

"Are they trying to cure your immortality or replicate it?"

I turned to look at her. "What do you mean? Cure it, of course."

"Really? If they don't want any change, wouldn't it

make sense to infect everyone with it?"

"It makes a perverse kind of sense, I suppose. If you were into conspiracy theories, it would be believable. But I know these guys—they don't have it in them to lie to me, or to make me sad on purpose. That's the good thing about living here: you can always be sure that the people around you are every bit as nice as they seem. Sincere."

"If you say so," she said. Even though she didn't have an antenna, I could feel her skepticism. Fine, be skeptical. Wireheads didn't scheme, they just *did stuff*, that was what it meant to be a wirehead. She nuzzled my neck. I turned my head and we kissed. It was weird with the lights on.

I broke it off and said, "I've got to get to the lab." The Flea was running in little circles and chiding me, making the point. I pulled on my jumpsuit and zipped it up.

"Will you be long?"

I shrugged. "Couple hours," I said. "Don't answer the door, OK? I mean, just lay low. Stay here. My neighbors—"

"I get it," she said. "Don't want to get kidnapped and wired up, right?"

"They won't kidnap you. Just put the question to you and kick you out if you give the wrong answer."

She opened her arms. "Come give me a kiss goodbye, my brave protector," she said. I leaned in and let her give me a hard hug and a harder kiss. The hug felt like that first night, when it was just the chance to have a human being holding me; the kiss felt like the night before, when we'd done things I'd never given much thought to.

"Love you, Jimmy," she whispered fiercely in my ear.

Dad used to say that a lot. "You too," I said, because it was what I always said to him.

○ ○ ○

The sun was high and the day was crisp, the kind of weather that made you forget just how hot it could be in the summer. Drifts of colored leaves rustled around me as the bare trees sighed in the wind. The sun was bright and harsh. I'd been through many of these autumns, but I'd never had a day that felt this *autumnal*, this crisp and real and vivid.

There were plenty of wireheads out and about. Some of them were driving transports filled with staple crops grown in our fields. Some were chatting with traders, who blew through town every day. Some were just sitting on a bench and smiling and nodding at the passers-by, which might as well be the cult's national sport.

They greeted me, one and all. Everyone knew me and no one asked me nosy questions about my . . . condition. Everyone knew enough to know that I was just the kid who wouldn't grow up, and that I could give them a fine show if they came and knocked on my door.

Normally that felt good. Today, it loomed over me, oppressing me. They'd all have heard about Lacey by now. They were seeing me walk down the street, so they knew that Lacey must be alone in the Carousel. They'd be thinking together, wondering about her, thinking about going over there to find out when she'd be signing up for her wire. And that was the one thing I *didn't* want. Lacey had managed to change over the past twenty years, becoming an adult, leaving behind Treehuggerism, having adventures. Turning into a woman. I didn't want her frozen in time the way we all were. *I* didn't want to be frozen in time anymore. Besides, she knew my secret now, that my antenna didn't work the way everyone else's did. If she became a wirehead, she'd tell them about it. She'd have to.

The labs had been in the old University bioscience building, but a trader had sold the researchers a self-assembling lab-template a couple years before. The wireheads had held a long congress about putting up a major building, but in the end, the researchers were made so clearly miserable by the prospect of not being able to put up a new building that they'd prevailed; the wireheads had caved in just to get them to cheer the hell up.

The new building looked like a giant heap of gelatinous frogspawn: huge, irregular bubbles in a jumble that spread wide and high. The template had taken in the disciplinary needs of the researchers and analyzed their communications patterns to come up with an optimal geometry for clustering research across disciplines and collaborative groupings. The researchers loved it—you could feel that just by getting close to the building—but no one else could make any sense of it, especially since the bubbles moved themselves around all the time as they sought new, higher levels of optimal configuration.

I could usually find my research group without much trouble. I climbed up a few short staircases, navigated around some larger labs filled with equipment that Dad would have loved, and eventually arrived at their door. There were three of them today: Randy, the geneticist; Inga, the endocrinologist; and Wen, the oncologist.

"You think it's cancer again, huh?"

Randy and Inga nodded gravely at Wen. "That's our best guess, Jimmy. It's the cheapest and easiest way to get cells to keep on copying themselves. We thought we'd try you out on some new anticancer from India." Inga was in her thirties; I'd played with her when she was my age. Now she seemed to see me as nothing more than a research subject.

Wen nodded and spread his hands out on the table. "We infiltrate your marrow with computational agents that do continuous realtime evaluation of your transcription activity, looking for anomalies, comparing the data-set to baseline subjects. Once we have a good statistical picture of what's happening, we intervene in anomalous transcriptions, correcting them. It's a simple approach, just brute force computation, but there's a new IIT nanoscale petaflop agent that raises the bar on what 'brute force' really means."

"And this works?"

They all looked at each other. I felt their discomfort distantly in my antenna. "It's had very successful animal trials."

"How about human trials?" I already knew the answer.

"Dr Chandrasekhar at IIT has asked us to serve as a test site for his human trials research. He was very impressed with your germ plasm. He's been culturing it for months." Randy was getting his geek back, a pure joy I could feel even through my muffled receiver. "You should see the stuff he's done with it. Your father—"

"A genius, I know." I didn't usually mind talking about Dad, but that day it felt wrong. I'd pictured him once, briefly, as Lacey and I had been together, and had zigged wrong and ended up bending myself at an awkward angle. It was the thought of what Dad would say if he caught me "deracinating."

"He didn't keep notes?"

"Not where I could get at them. He had a lot of friends around the world—they all worked on it. There's probably lots more like me, somewhere or other. He told me he'd let me in once I was old enough."

"Probably worried about being generation-gapped," Randy said sagely.

"I don't get it," I said.

"You know. Whatever he'd done to himself, you were decades further down the line. If he'd kept up what he was doing, and if you'd joined him, you'd have been able to do it again, make a kid who was way more advanced than you. You'd end up living forever like a caveman among your genius superman descendants. So he wanted to keep the information from you." He shrugged. "That's what Chandrasekhar says, anyway. He's done a lot of research on immortality cabals. He didn't know about your dad's, though. He was very impressed."

"So you said." I hadn't really thought about this before. Dad was—Dad. He was all-seeing, all-knowing, all-powerful. He hadn't just fathered me, he'd *designed* me. Of course, he'd designed me to patch all the bugs in his own genome, but—

"So as I said, we've cultured a lot of your plasm and run this on it. What we get looks like normal aging. Mitochondrial shortening. Maturity."

"How big a culture?" I was raised by a gifted bioscientist. I knew which questions to ask.

"Several billion cells," Inga said, with a toss of her hair. I could feel their discomfort again, worse than before.

"Right . . ." I did some mental arithmetic. "So, like, a ten-centimeter square of skin?"

The three of them grinned identical, sheepish grins. "It scales," Inga said. "There's a four-hundred-kilo gorilla running it right now. Stable for a year. Rock solid."

I shook my head. "I don't think so," I said. "I mean, it's very exciting and all, but I've already been a guinea pig once, when I was born. Let someone else go first this time."

They all looked at each other. I felt the dull throb of their anxiety. They looked at me.

"We've been looking for someone else to trial this on, but there's no one else with your special—" Wen groped for the word.

"There has to be," I said. "Dad didn't invent me on his own. There was a whole team of them. They all wanted to make their contributions. There's probably whole cities full of immortal adolescents out there somewhere."

"If we could find them, we'd ask them. But no one we know has heard of them. Chandrasekhar has put the word out everywhere. He swings a big stick. He said to ask if you know where your dad's friends lived?"

"Dad had a huge fight with those people when I was born, some kind of schism. I never saw him communicating with them."

"And your mother?"

"Dead. I told you. When I was an infant. Don't remember her, either." I swallowed and got my temper under control. Someday, someone was going to notice that even when I looked all pissed off, my antenna wasn't broadcasting anything and I'd be in for it. They'd probably split me open and stick five more in me. Or tie me naked to a tree and leave me there as punishment for deceiving them. It's amazing how cruel you can be when there's a whole city full of people who'll soak up your conscience and smooth it out for you.

"Chandrasekhar says—"

"I'm getting a little tired of hearing about him. What is it? Is it ego? You want to impress this big-shot doctor from the civilized east, prove to him that we're not just a bunch of bumpkins here? We *are* a bunch of bumpkins here, guys. We live in the woods! That's the *point*. What do you think *they'd* all say if they knew you were trying this?" I waved my arm in an expansive gesture, taking in the whole town. I knew what it was like to have a dirty little secret around there, and I knew I'd get them with that.

Inga's face clouded over. "Listen to me, Jimmy. You started this. You came to us and asked us to investigate this. To cure you. It's not our fault that answering your question took us to places you never anticipated. We're busy people. There are plenty of other things we could be doing. We all have to do our part."

The other two were flinching away from the sear of her emotion. I did what any wirehead would do when confronted with such a blast: I left.

o o o

There was a small crowd hanging around the Carousel as I got back to it. They weren't exactly blocking the way, more like milling about, chatting, being pastoral, but always in the vicinity of my home. Someone came out of my outhouse: Brent. A moment later, I spotted Sebastien.

"We were hoping for a ride," he said. "Brent was asking about it again."

Uh-huh. "And these other people?"

My antenna wasn't radiating sarcasm or anger, though my voice was full of both. He believed the evidence of his antenna and continued to treat me as though I was calm and quiet.

"Other riders, I suppose."

"Well, I'm not giving any rides today," I said. "You can all go home."

"Is it broken again?"

"No," I said.

"Oh," he said.

Brent and Tina wandered up. Brent looked at me with his head cocked to one side. "Hi, Jimmy," he said. "We want to go inside and ride around."

"Not today. Try me again in a week."

Tina put a hand on my arm. It was warm and maternal. It made me feel weird. "Jimmy, you know you have to bring her around to council if she's going to stay here. It's the way we do things."

"She's not staying," I said.

"She's stayed long enough. We can't ignore it, you know. It's not fair for you to ask us to pretend we didn't see her. We all have a duty. Your friend can get the operation, or she can go."

"She's not staying," I said. *Neither am I* is what I didn't say.

"Jimmy," she said, but I didn't want to hear what she had to say. I shook off her arm and climbed the ramp up to my door, sliding it aside, stepping in quickly and sliding it shut behind me.

"Look, I'm a nest!" The entire pack had swarmed Lacey, perching on her arms, head, shoulders and chest. She was sitting in the front row of the theater, balancing. "These are some fun little critters. I can't believe they lived this long!"

I shrugged. "Far as I can tell, they're immortal." I shrugged again. "Poor little fuckers."

She shook off the pack. They raced around under the seats. They were starting to get squirrelly. I really should have been taking them out for walks more often. She came and gathered me in her arms. It felt good, and weird.

"What's going on?"

"Let's go, OK? The two of us."

"You don't mean out for a walk, do you?"

"No."

She let go of me and sat on the stage. We were in the "future" set, which Dad said was about 1989, but not very accurate for all that. The lights on the Christmas tree twinkled. I'd wiki-tagged everything in the room, and the entry on Christmas trees had been deeply disturbing to me. All that *family* stuff. So . . . treehugger. Some of the wireheads did Christmas, but no one ever invited me along, thankfully.

"I don't think that's a good idea, Jimmy. It's dangerous out there."

"I can handle danger." I swallowed. "I've killed people, you know. That last day I saw you, when they came for Detroit. I killed eight of them. I'm not a kid."

"No, you're not a kid. But you are, too. I don't know, Jimmy." She sighed and looked away. "I'm sorry about last night. I never should have—"

"*I'm not a kid!* I'm older than you are—just because I look like this doesn't mean I'm not thirty-two, you know. It doesn't mean I'm not capable of love." I realized what I'd just said.

"Jimmy, I didn't mean it like that. But whatever you are, we can't be, you know, a couple. You can see that, right? For God's sake, Jimmy, we're not even the same species!"

It felt like she'd punched me in the chest. The air went out of my lungs and I stared at her, pop-eyed, for a long moment.

I felt tears prick at my eyes and I realized how childish they'd make me seem, and I held them back, letting only one choked snuffle escape. Then I nodded, calmly.

"Of course. I didn't want to be part of any kind of couple with you. Just a traveling companion. But I can take care of myself. It's fine."

She shook her head. I could see that she had tears in *her* eyes, but it didn't seem childish when she did it. "That's not what I meant, Jimmy. Please understand me—"

"I understand. Last night was a mistake. We're not the same species. You don't want to travel with me. It's not hard to understand."

"It's not like that—"

"Sure. It's much nicer than that. There are a million nice things you can say about me and about this that will show me that it's really not about me, it's just a kind of emergent property of the universe with no one to blame. I understand perfectly."

She bit her lip.

"That's it, huh?"

She didn't say anything. She shook her head.

"So? What did I get wrong, then?"

Without saying another word, she fled.

I went outside a minute later. My neighbors were radiating curiosity. No one asked me anything about the woman who'd run out of the Carousel and taken off. Her stuff was still in my little sleeping-space and leaned up against the stage. I packed it as neatly as I could and set it by the door. She could come and get it whenever she wanted.

o o o

The fourth scene in the Carousel of Progress is that late-eighties sequence. We had other versions of it in the archives, but the eighties one always appealed to Dad, so that was the one that I kept running most of the time.

Like I said, it's Christmastime, and there's a bunch of primitive "new" technology on display—a terrible video game, an inept automatic cooker, a laughable console. The whole family sits around and jokes and plays. Grandpa and Grandma are vigorous, independent. Sister and Brother are handsome young adults. Mom and Dad are a little older, wearing optical prostheses. Dad accidentally misprograms the oven and the turkey is scorched. Everyone laughs and they send out for pizza.

I always found that scene calming. It was supposed to be set a little in the future, to inspire the audience to see the great big beautiful tomorrow, shining at the end of every day (for a while, the theme of the ride had been, "Now is the best time of your life," which seemed to me to be a little more realistic—who knew what tomorrow would be like?).

Dad believed in progress, I've come to realize. He made me because he thought that the human race would supplanted by something transhuman, beyond human. Like it would go, squirrel, monkey, ape, caveman, human, me. He was the missing link between the last two steps, the human who'd been modded into transhumanism.

But if Dad were alive today, he'd probably be learning from his mistakes with me and making a 2.0 version. Someone who made me look as primitive as I made Dad look. And twenty years after 2.0, there'd be a 3.0, a whole generation more advanced. Maybe twenty feet tall and able to grow extra limbs at will.

And in a thousand years, we'd still be alive, weird, immortal cavemen surrounded by our telepathic, shapeshifting, hyperintelligent descendants.

Progress.

o o o

I heard Lacey let herself in on the second night. I'd lain awake all night the first night, waiting for her to come back for her bedroll and her cowl. When she didn't, I figured she'd found somewhere warm to stay. There had been a lot of treehouse seed in the air for the past four or five years, and the saplings were coming up now, huge, hollow root-balls protruding from the ground. They grew very fast, like all good carbon-sinking projects, but they had a tendency to out-compete the local species, so the wireheads chopped them down and mulched them when they took root. Still, you didn't have to go very far into our woods to find one.

I spent the next day paying social calls on wireheads, letting their talk about crops and trade while away the hours, just spending the time away from home so I wouldn't have to see Lacey if she came back for her things that day. But when I came home and said hello to the pack and made dinner, her pack was still by the door. At that point, I decided she wouldn't come back for a while. Maybe she'd found a nice traveler to go caravanning with.

She let herself in quietly, but the pack was roused, and a second later I was roused too. My bedding still smelled like her. I was going to have to wash it. Or maybe burn it.

I sat up and padded through the gloom into the fourth scene. She was sitting in a middle-row aisle seat with her pack between her knees, watching the silent silhouettes of the robots in their Christmas living room.

I shrugged and turned it on. We watched them burn the turkey. They ordered out for pizza. They sang: "There's a great big beautiful tomorrow/shining at the end of every day." The Carousel rotated another 60 degrees and back to the beginning. The show ended.

"Safe travels," I said to her.

She rocked in her seat as if I'd slapped her. "Jimmy, I have something I need to tell you. About that day in Detroit. Something I couldn't tell you before." She took a shuddering breath.

"You have to understand. I didn't know what my parents were planning. They didn't like you any more than your dad liked me, so I was a little suspicious when they told me to take my spidergoat and go and play with you over in the city. But things had been really tense around the house and we'd just had another blazing fight and I figured they wanted to have a discussion without me around and so they told me to do the thing that would be sure to distract me.

"I didn't realize that they wanted me to distract you, too.

"They told me later that someone else had gone into town to lure your father away, too. The idea was the get both of you away from your defenses, to demolish your capacity to attack, and then to turn the wumpuses loose on the city until there was nothing left, then to let you go. But your dad got away, figured out what was going on, got into his plane and—"

She shut her mouth. I looked at her, letting this sink in, waiting for some words to come.

"They told me this later, you understand. Weeks later. Long after you were gone. I had no idea. They had friends in Buffalo who had the mechas and the flying platform, friends who were ideologically committed to getting rid of the old cities. They hated your dad. He had lots of enemies. They didn't tell me until afterward, though. I was just . . . bait."

I remembered how fast she had disappeared when the bombs started falling. And not into the mecha, which should have been the safest place of all. No, she'd gone out of the city.

"You knew," I said.

She wiped her eyes. "What?"

"You *knew*. That's why you scarpered so quickly. That's why you didn't get into the mecha. You knew that they were coming for us. You knew you had to get out of the city."

"Jimmy, no—"

"Lacey, yes." The calm I felt was frightening. The pack twined around my feet, nervously. "You knew. You knew, you knew, you knew. Have you convinced yourself that you didn't know?"

"No," she said, putting her hands in front of her. "Jimmy, you don't understand. If I knew, why would I have come back here to confess?"

"Guilt," I said. "Regret. Anger with your parents. You were just a kid, right? Even if you knew, they still tricked you. They were still supposed to be protecting you, not using you to lure me away. Maybe you have a crush on me. Maybe you just want to screw with my head. Maybe you've just been distracting me while someone comes in to attack the wireheads."

She gave a shiver when I said that, a little violent shake like the one I did at the end of a piss. I saw, very clearly in the footlights from the stage, her pupils contracting.

"Wait," I said. "Wait, you're here to attack the *wire-heads*? Jesus Christ, Lacey, what the hell is wrong with you? They're the most harmless, helpless bunch of farmers in the world. Christ, they're practically Treehuggers, but without the stupid politics."

She got up and grabbed her pack. "I understand why you'd be paranoid, Jimmy, but this isn't fair. I'm just here to make things right between us—"

"Well, forgive me," I said. "What could I possibly have been thinking? After all, you were only just skulking around here, gathering intelligence, slipping off into the night. After all, you only have a history of doing this. After all, it's only the kind of thing you've been doing since you were a little girl—"

"Goodbye, Jimmy," she said. "You have a nice life, all right?"

She went out into the night. My chest went up and down like a bellows. My hands were balled into fists so tight it made my arms shake. The pack didn't like it. "Follow her," I whispered to Ike and Mike, the best trackers in the pack. "Follow her"—a command they knew well enough. I'd used them to spy on my neighbors after arriving here, getting the lay of the land. "Follow her," I said again, and they disappeared out the door, silent and swift.

I could watch and record their sensorium from my console. I packed a bag, keeping one eye on it as I went. I grabbed the pack's canisters. They were too heavy to carry, but I had a little wagon for them. I piled them on the wagon, watching its suspension sag under the weight.

Ike and Mike had her trail. She headed into the woods with the uneasy gait of a weeping woman, but gradually she straightened out. She kept on walking, picking up speed, clipping on an infrared pince-nez when she came under the canopy into the real dark. I noted it and messaged Ike and Mike about their thermal signatures. They fell back and upped the zoom on their imaging, the picture going a little shaky as they struggled to stabilize the camera at that magnification.

She emerged from the woods into a clearing heaped high with rubble. I watched her sit down with her feet under her, facing it. She was saying something. I moved Ike up into mic range. She didn't say much, though, and by the time he was in range, she fell silent.

The rubble stirred. Some rocks skittered down the side of the pile. Then a tentacle whipped out of the pile, a still-familiar mouth at the end of it. The mouth twisted around and grabbed up one of the larger rocks and began to digest it. More tentacles appeared, five, then fifty, then hundreds. The rubble shifted and revealed the wumpus beneath it.

It was the biggest one I'd ever seen. It had been twenty years since I'd last seen one of those bastards, and maybe my memories were faulty but this one seemed different. Meaner. Smarter. Wumpuses were usually bumblers, randomwalking and following concentration gradients for toxins, looking for cities to eat, mostly blind. This one unfolded itself and moved purposefully around the clearing, its wheels spinning and grinding. As it rolled, smaller wumpuses fell out of its hopper. It was . . . spawning!

It seemed to sense Ike and Mike's presence, turning between one and the other. They were deep in the woods, running as cold as possible, camouflaged, perfectly still, communicating via narrow, phased-array signals. They should be undetectable. Nevertheless, I gave them the order to shut down comms and pull back slowly to me.

I stood out on the porch, waiting for them to rejoin me in the dark, hearing the sounds of the night woods, the wind soughing through the remaining leaves, the sounds of small animals scampering in the leaves and the distant frying-bacon sound of the wumpus and its litter digesting.

There was no chance that Lacey was doing something good with that wumpus. She had lied from the minute she met me in the woods. She had scouted out the wirehead city. She had gone back and reported to some kind of highly evolved descendant of the wumpuses that ate every city on the continent.

I had already been ready to go. I could just follow through on my plan, hit the road and never look back. The wireheads weren't my people, just people I'd lived with.

If I was a better person, my instinct would be to stay and warn them. Maybe to stay and fight. The wumpus would need fighting, I knew that much.

I'm not a good person. I just wanted to go.

I didn't go—and not because I'm a good person. I didn't go because I needed to see Inga and find out if she really had the cure for my immortality.

○ ○ ○

Inga lived in the same house she'd grown up in. I'd gone over to play there, twenty years ago. Her parents had just grown new rooms as their kids had grown up, married, and needed more space. Now their place had ramified in all directions, with outbuildings and half-submerged cellars. I took a chance that Inga's room would be where it had been the last time.

I knocked on the door, softly at first. Then louder.

The man who answered the door was old and grey. His pajamas flapped around him in the wind that whipped through the autumn night. He scrubbed at his eyes and looked at me.

"Can I help you?" His antenna radiated his peevish sleepiness.

"Inga," I said. My heart was hammering in my chest and the sweat of my exertions, lugging the pack's canisters across town, was drying in the icy wind, making me shiver. "I need to see Inga."

"You know what time it is?"

"Please," I said. "I'm one of her research subjects. It's urgent."

He shook his head. The irritation intensified. With all the other wireheads asleep, there was no one to damp his emotion. I wondered if he was souring their dreams with his bad vibes.

"She's in there," he said, pointing to another outbuilding, smaller and farther away from the main house. I thanked him and pulled my wagon over to Inga's door.

She answered the door in a nightshirt and a pair of heavy boots. Her hair was in a wild halo around her head and limned by the light behind her and I had a moment where I realized that she was very beautiful, something that had escaped me until then.

"Jimmy?" she said, peering at me. "Christ, Jimmy—"

"Can I come in?"

"What's this about?"

"Can I come in?"

She stood aside. I felt her irritation, too.

Her room was small and crowded with elaborate sculpture made from fallen branches wound with twine. Some of them were very good. It was a side of her I'd never suspected. Weirdly enough, being a wirehead didn't seem to diminish artistic capacity—there were some very good painters and even a couple of epic poets in the cult that I quite liked.

"You know that there's been a woman staying with me?"

She made a face. "It's not any of my business, and I don't really have any romantic advice—"

I cut her off. I told her everything. Even the sex parts. Even the antenna parts. Especially the wumpus parts. For such a big load of secrets, it didn't take long to impart.

"So you think she'll attack the city?"

I suppressed my own irritation—maybe it was the dull reflection of hers. "I know she will." I took out my console and showed her the pictures of the wumpus.

"So you're telling me this. Why? Why not wake up someone important? Someone who can help us?"

"I don't think there's any helping us. You saw it. You saw its babies. It's coming for us, soon. This place is all over. I don't know if it eats people, but it's going to eat everything human-made here. That's what they do."

I felt her draw strength and calm from the sleeping people around us, from the whole city, dissipating her fear through the network.

"So why *are* you here?"

"I want you to give me the Chandrasekhar treatment before I go."

"You're leaving?"

I gestured at my wagon.

"And you want the cure? Yesterday you didn't want to be a guinea pig."

"Yesterday I thought there'd be a tomorrow. Now I'm not so sure. I want the cure."

She folded her arms and stared at me.

"Your antenna isn't totally dead, you know," she said at last. "I can sort of feel a little of what you're feeling. It's too bad it doesn't work better. That's not a good way to feel."

"You'll do it?"

"Why not? It's the end of the world, apparently."

o o o

The sound of frying bacon filled the night as we worked in her lab. We dilated the windows at first, so we could track the progress of the wumpuses through town. There were a lot of angry shouts and sobs, but nothing that sounded like screams of pain. The wumpuses were apparently eating the buildings and leaving the people, just as they had two decades before.

The procedure was surprisingly simple—mostly it was just installing some code on my console and then a couple of shots from a long, thin bone-needle. That hurt, but less than I expected. I made sure I had the source-code as well as the object-code in case I needed to debug anything: the last thing I wanted was to be unable to manage my system.

We watched in fascination as statistical data about my transcriptions began to fill the screens around us. The app came with some statistically normal data-sets that overlaid the visualizations of my own internal functionality. It was clear even to my eye that I was pretty goddamned weird down there at the cellular level.

"What happens now?"

"The thing wants a full two month's worth of data before it starts doing anything. So basically, you run that for a couple of months, and then it should prompt you for permission to intervene in your transcriptions to make them more normal."

"Two months? That must suck if you've got cancer."

"Cancer might kill you in two months and it might not. Bad nanites messing with your cellular activity is a lot scarier."

"I've been trying not to think of that," I said.

The frying bacon noises were growing louder.

"No more shouts," Inga said. Her eyes were big and round. "What do you think is going on out there?"

I shook my head. "I'm an idiot, give me a second."

I gathered the pack in my arms and gave them their instructions, then tossed them out the window. They scampered down the building side and I fired up the console.

"There," I said, pointing. The wumpuses were moving in a long curved line now, a line as wide as the town, curving up like a pincer at the edges. They moved slowly and deliberately through the night. Pepe found a spot where they were working their way through a block of flats, tentacles whipping back and forth, great plumes of soil arcing out behind them. People ran out of the house, carrying their belongings, shouting at the wumpuses, throwing rocks at them. The wumpuses took no notice, save to snatch the thrown rocks out of the air and drop them into their hoppers.

An older man—I recognized him as Emmanuel, one of the real village elders around here—moved around to confront the wumpus that was eating his house. He shouted more words at it, then took another step toward it.

One of the tentacles moved faster than I'd ever seen a wumpus go. It whipped forward and snatched Emmanuel up by the torso and lifted him high in the air. Before he could make a sound, it had plunged him headfirst into its hopper. One of his legs kicked out, just once, before he disappeared.

The other wireheads around him were catching the fear, spread by the wires, too intense to damp down. They screamed and ran and the wumpuses picked them up, one after another, seeming to blindly triangulate on the sounds of their voices. Each one went headfirst into the hopper. Each one vanished.

I stood up and whistled the pack back to me.

I moved for the door. Inga blocked my way.

"Where are you going?"

"Away," I said. I thought for a moment. "You can come if you want."

She looked at me and I realized that what I'd always mistaken for pity was really a kind of disgust. Why not? I was the neighbor kid who'd never grown up. It *was* disgusting.

"You brought her here," she said, quietly. I wondered from the tone of her voice if she meant to kill me, even though she'd just treated me.

"She came here," I said. "I had nothing to do with it. Just a coincidence. Sit in one place for twenty years and everyone you've ever known will cross your path. Whatever she's doing, it's nothing to do with me. I explained that."

Inga slumped into a lab-chair.

"Are you coming?" I asked.

She cried. I'd never heard a wirehead cry. Either there wasn't enough mass in the wirehead network to absorb her emotion or the prevailing mood was complete despair. I stood on the threshold, holding my wagon filled with the pack's canisters. I reached out and grabbed her hand and tugged at it. She jerked it away. I tried again and she got off her stool and stalked deeper into labs.

That settled it.

I left, pulling my wagon behind me.

∘ ∘ ∘

The sound of frying bacon was everywhere. I had the pack running surveillance patterns around me, scouting in all directions, their little squirrel cases eminently suited to this kind of thing. We were a team, my pack and me. We could keep it up for days before their batteries needed recharging. I'd topped up the nutrients in their canisters before leaving the Carousel.

The frying bacon sound had to include the destruction of the Carousel. Every carefully turned replacement part, all those lines of code. The mom and the dad and the son and the sister and the grandparents and their doggies. Dad's most precious prize, gone to wumpusdust.

The sound of frying bacon was all around us. The sound of screams. Lacey had arrived from the west. To the east was the ocean. I would go south, where it was warm and where, if the world was coming to an end, I would at least not freeze to death.

There was a column of refugees on the southbound roadway, the old Route 40. I steered clear of them and crashed through the woods instead, the wagon's big tires and suspension no match for the uneven ground, so that I hardly moved at all.

The pack raced ahead and behind me, playing lookout. They were excited, scared. I could still hear the screams. Sometimes a wirehead would plunge past me in the night, charging through the woods.

The wumpus came on me without warning. It was small, small enough to have nuzzled through the trees without knocking them aside. Maybe as tall as me, not counting those whiplike tentacles, not counting the mouths on the end of them, mouths that opened and shut against the moonlight sky in silhouette.

I remembered all those wumpuses I'd killed one tentacle at a time. These wumpuses seemed a lot smarter than the ones I'd known in Detroit. Someone must have kludged them up. I wondered if they knew how I'd played with their ancestors. I wondered if Lacey had told them.

Wumpuses only have rudimentary vision. Their keenest sense is chemical, an ability to follow concentration gradients of inorganic matter, mindlessly groping their way to food sources. They have excellent hearing, as well. I stood still and concentrated on not smelling inorganic.

The wumpus's tentacles danced in the sky over me. Then moving as one, the pack leapt for them.

The pack's squirrel bodies looked harmless and cute, but they had retractable claws that could go through concrete, and teeth that could tear your throat out. The basic model was used for antipersonnel military defense.

The wumpus recoiled from the attack and its tentacles flailed at the angry little doggies that were mixed among its roots, trying to pick them off even as they uprooted tentacle after tentacle.

I cheered silently and pulled the wagon away as fast as I could. I looked over my shoulder in time to see one of my doggies get caught up in a mouth and tossed into the hopper, vanishing into a plume of dust. That was OK—I could get them new bodies, provided that I could just get their canisters away with me.

I tugged the wagon, feeling like my arm would come off, feeling like my heart would burst my chest. I had superhuman strength and endurance, but it wasn't infinite.

In the end, I was running blind, sweat soaking my clothes, eyes down on the trail ahead of me, moving in any direction that took me away from the frying bacon sound.

Then, in an instant, the wagon was wrenched out of my hand. I grabbed for it with my stiff arm, turning around, stumbling. There was another wumpus there, holding the wagon aloft in two of its mouths. The canisters tumbled free, bouncing on the forest floor. The wumpus caught three of them on the first bounce, triangulating on the sound. I watched helplessly as it tossed my brave, immortal, friends into its hopper, digesting them.

Then the fourth canister rolled away and I chased after it, snatching at it, but my fingertips missed it. A hand reached out of the dark and snatched it up. I followed the hand back into the shadows.

"Oh, Jimmy," Lacey said.

I leapt for her, fingers outstretched, going for the throat.

She sidestepped, tripped me with one neat outstretched foot, then lifted me to my feet by my collar. I grabbed for the canister, the last of my friends, and she casually flipped it into the wumpus's hopper.

A spray of dust coated us. The plume. My friend.

I began to cry.

"Jimmy," she said, barely loud enough to be heard over the frying bacon. "You don't understand, Jimmy. They're safe now. It's copying them. Copying everything. That's what we never understood about the wumpuses. They're making copies of the things that they eat."

She set me down and grabbed me by the shoulders. "It's OK, Jimmy. Your friends are safe now, forever. They can never die now. The wireheads, too."

I stared into her eyes. I'd loved her. She was quite mad.

"What do you get out of it?"

"What did your father get out of what he did? He made one child immortal. We'll save the world. The whole world." She smiled at me, like she expected me to smile back. I smiled back and she relaxed her grip on my arms. That's when I clapped her ears, cupping my hands like I'd been taught to do if I wanted to rupture her eardrums. Dad liked to work through self-defense videos with me.

She went down with a shout and I stepped on her stomach as I clambered over her and ran, ran, ran.

PART 3: THERE'LL ALWAYS BE THE GOOD GUYS SHOOTIN' IT OUT WITH THE BAD GUYS

I USED TO DRIVE MECHAS for joyriding. Now it's a medical necessity.

I piloted my suit down the Keys, going amphibious and sinking to the ocean-bottom rather than risk the bridges. The bridges were where the youth gangs hung out, eyes luminous and hard. You never knew when they'd swarm you and mindrape you.

I hated the little bastards.

The Second Wumpus Devastation had destroyed—or preserved, if you preferred—every hominid in the Keys, and taken down every human-made structure. Today, we survivors lived in treehouses and ate breadberries.

Looking at old maps, I can see that my treehouse is right in the middle of the site of the old KOA Campground on Sugarloaf key. I like it for the proximity to Haiti, where an aggressive military culture kept the island wumpus-free and hence in possession of several generations of functional mechas. There were a few years there, after I escaped from the wireheads and the wumpuses, when I grew into a strapping buck and was able to earn one of these lethal little bastards by serving in an antiwumpus militia.

"Earn" is probably the wrong word. The youth gangs wiped out the militias a few years into my stint. You'd be out on patrol and then a group of these kids would glide out of the bush so silent it was like they were on rails. They'd surround you, hypnotizing you with those eyes of theirs, with those *antennae* of theirs, and you'd be frozen like a mouse pinned by a cobra's gaze. They'd SQUID you right through your armor, dropping the superconducting quantum field around your head, ripping through your life, your deep structures, your secrets and habits, making a record for the cloud, or wherever it was all the data went to.

After a thorough mindraping, hard militiamen would be reduced to shell-shocked existential whiners, useless for combat. They'd abandon their powered suits and wander off into the bush, end up in some taproom, drinking to forget the void they faced as their brains were spooled out like an archival tape being transferred to modern media.

I'd been caught out one day, the air-conditioner wheezing to keep my naked flesh cool in the form-fitting cradle of the mecha. The mecha was only twice as tall as me, practically child-sized compared to the big ones we'd had in Detroit, and it was cranky and balky. I could pick up an egg with Dad's mecha and not break the shell. The force-feedback manipulators in this actually *clicked* through a series of defined settings, click-click-click, the mecha's hands opening and closing in a clittery clatter like a puppet's.

I waded through the swampy bush, navigating by the wumpusplume on the horizon. Somewhere, a couple clicks away, something was converting one of Florida's precious remaining human-made structures into soil—and taking the humans along with it. No one knew if the wumpuses and the youth gangs were on the same side. No one knew if there were "sides." The first gen of wumpuses had been made by a half-dozen agrarian cultists on the west coast. They'd been modded and hacked by any number of tinkerers who'd captured them, decompiled them, and improved them. I hear that the first could generations actually came with source-code and a makefile, which must have been handy.

They stepped out of the brush in unison. It took an eyeblink. They were utterly silent.

And a little familiar.

They were me. Me, during that long, long pre-adolescence, when I was ageless and lived among the wireheads.

Oh, not exactly. There were minor variations in their facial features. Some wore their hair long and shaggy. Others kept it short. One had freckles. One was black. Two might have been Latino.

But they were also *me*. They looked like brothers to one another, and they looked like my own brothers. I can't explain it better than that: I knew they were me the same way I knew that the guy I saw in my shaving mirror was me.

They surrounded my mecha in a rough circle and closed in on me. They looked at me and I looked at them, rotating my mecha's cockpit through a full 360. I'd always assumed that they came out of a lab somewhere, like the wumpuses. But up close, you could see that they'd been dressed at some point: some had been dressed in precious designer kids' clothes, others in hand-me-down rags. Some bore the vestiges of early allegiance to one subculture or another: implanted fashion-lumps that ridged their faces and arms, glittering bits of metal and glass sunk into their flesh and bones. These young men hadn't been hatched: they'd been born, raised, and *infected*.

They made eye contact without flinching. I fought a bizarre urge to wave at them, to get out of the mecha and talk to them. It was that recognition.

Then they raised their hands in unison and I knew that the mindrape was coming. I braced against it. The fields apparently came from implanted generators. They had the stubs of directional antennae visible behind their left ears, just as the stories said. I felt a buzzing, angry feeling, emanating from the vestiges of my wirehead antenna, like a toothache throughout my whole head.

I waited for it to intensify. I didn't think I could move. I tried. My hand twitched a little, but not enough to reach my triggers. I don't know if I could have killed them anyway.

The rape would come, I knew it. And I was helpless against it. I struggled with my own body, but all I could accomplish was the barest flick of an eye, the tiniest movement of a fingertip.

Then they broke off. My arm shot forward to my controls, my knuckles mashing painfully into the metal over the buttons. An inch lower and I would have mown them down where they stood. Maybe it would have killed them.

They backed away slowly, moving back into the woods. If I had been mindraped, it had been painless and nearly instantaneous, nothing like the descriptions I'd heard.

I watched the gang member directly ahead of me melt back into the brush, and I put the mecha's tracers on him, stuck it on autopilot, and braced myself. These mechas used millimeter-wave radar and satellite photos to map their surroundings and they'd chase anything you told them to, climbing trees, leaping obstacles. They weren't gentle about it, either: the phrase "stealthy mecha" doesn't exist in any human language. It thundered through the marshy woods, splashing and crashing and leaping as I jostled in my cocoon and focused on keeping my lunch down.

The kid was fast and seemed to have an intuitive grasp of how to fake out the mecha's algorithms. He used the water to his great advantage, stepping on slippery logs over bog-holes that my mecha stepped into a second later, mired in stinky, sticky mud. Once I got close enough to him to see the grime on the back of his neck and count the mosquito bites on his cheek, but then he slipped away, darting into a burrow hole as my mecha's fingers clicked behind him.

That night, I returned to camp and found that only three other militiamen had made it back, out of eighteen. I climbed out of my mecha and we did a little of the weird yoga they'd taught us in basic to get our bodies back after being trapped immobile in a rubber, form-fitting suit for eight hours in the mecha. None of us spoke of the day. We knew what had happened to our comrades. Some of them had been my friends. One, a pretty Haitian girl named Monique, had been my lover. She'd been teaching me French. We knew we could find them by canvassing the nearby bars. They'd be spending the last of their money, drinking and crying until the money ran out. We'd next see them begging on a street, tears slipping down their cheeks.

I didn't tell them about being caught by the youth gang, nor about the unsuccessful mindrape. I certainly didn't tell them about seeing myself in the faces of the youth gang.

By the morning, there were only two of us left. Grad,

a taciturn older man, had left his mecha but taken his pack. I wished him good luck.

I looked into the eyes of the remaining militiaman. Technically, he was my superior, having the pip that made him into a nominal corporal. But Marcus wasn't really non-com material, didn't like making eye contact. Didn't like conflict. He'd been promoted for valor in the field after losing it on a bunch of wumpuses and taking down like thirty in an afternoon, while they flailed at him. When we'd pried him, shaking, out of his mecha, his eyes were still lit up like glowbugs, and he had a huge, throbbing boner.

Marcus ticked a salute off his forehead at me, then grabbed his own pack and walked off. That left me alone. The sounds of the forest were loud around me. Mosquitoes bit at my neck and whined in my ears. I climbed into my mecha and clomped off, but not on my patrol route: I headed south, down to the Keys, making an executive decision to take an extended scouting trip into unknown territory. Without any particular plan to return.

OK, so I stole the mecha. I also never got my last three pay-packets. Let's call it even.

o o o

Good thing I did, too. I found a grey hair in my eyebrow within a week. Within a month, the hair on my chest had gone white and the wrinkles had spread from the corners of my eyes to the tops of my arms. Six months later, I needed a cane. Within a year, it was two canes.

It was the stuff in my marrow, of course. All those borrowed years, undone with a single injection. I tried to shut them down using the console, but they weren't responding. I presumed that somewhere—Chennai, maybe—some colleague of Chandrasekhar would be fascinated to hear about this. Someone who'd love to know about the long-term outcomes in his experiment.

Being the long-term outcome was less fun.

I piloted my mecha up the walls of the treehouse on Sugarloaf Key. The bottom floors have something wrong with them, some mutant gene that caused their furnishings to extrude from the ceiling and walls. The upper floors were all right, though, and I have very simple needs.

Climbing out of the mecha gets harder every day. Just looking at my body gets harder, to tell the truth. The wrinkles, the liver spots, the swollen joints. My physical age is impossible to guess, but I feel like I'm 120, a skeleton wrapped in papery skin. Every vein stands out, every bone, every joint.

I inched down the limb of the treehouse and into my room. I had a little air-breathing radio-oven and a narrow bed padded with dried boughs from the tree. There was a comfortable sofa that I'd improved with a couple big pillows. It was more than I needed. By the time I got home from a day's foraging, there wasn't anything to do except choke down a little food and rest my bones until my bladder got me up, which it did, like clockwork, every two hours, all night long. There are lots of things I try not to dwell upon. The fact that this is all my fault is one of those things.

It was later that night, the third or fourth time I stumbled to the oubliette for yet another piss, that some sound caught me and brought me to the door. I'm not sure what it was: nighttimes are a riot of ocean noises, animal sounds, insect sounds, wind soughing through the boughs. Something was different that night. I took up my canes and tottered to the door, leaning on the jamb.

My mecha stood before me, cheap and nasty and lethal, a silhouette in the moonlight. I looked out into the woods, I looked down at the floor, and finally I looked up.

He was sitting on one of the high, thin branches of my treehouse. He was wearing loose pantaloons that hung in folds around his legs, a tight zippered jacket, and a confusion of rings and necklaces. It was dark and he was all in shades of grey, except for his luminous white face, peering at me from his hood and his halo of elaborately braided hair.

"Hello there," he said. He seemed to be on the verge of laughing at some private joke, and somehow I knew that I wasn't the butt of it. "Sorry to wake you. We have business to discuss. Can I come in?"

I looked up at him, squinting. I thought about toggling the floodlights on my mecha but decided that whatever he wanted, I wasn't in a position to deny it to him. Out of my mecha, I was helpless. He could knock me over with a puff of air.

I backed away from the door, leaning on my canes, and jerked my chin at the insides of my place. "Guess so," I said.

I struggled into a pair of shorts before hitting the lights. His pupils dilated with the telltale snap of night-vision enhancements, so the shorts were redundant. He'd already seen everything. What did I have to be modest about anyway?

He was tall and thin, his hair a mad ash-blond dandelion clock around his face. He had a foxlike chin and nose, and a wide mouth that curled up at the corners in a profusion of dimples, making his smile look like a caricature.

"Would you like tea?" I asked. It helped me sleep sometimes, so I was in the habit of making tea in the middle of the night.

"You make it with those chanterelles you pick?"

I narrowed my eyes at him. "You know a lot about me."

"It's not really tea at that point. More like consommé. But I'll try some."

I put the dried mushrooms in my tea egg and dropped it into a jar of water from the treehouse's condenser, then stuck it in the cooker, letting it figure out the timing and all.

"You know a lot about me," I said again.

"I know a lot about you," he agreed. He sat down on the edge of my bed. "I helped design you, if you want to know the truth. I knew your parents."

I looked more closely at him. He barely seemed a day over thirty. So he was telling me that he was an immortal, then. About time I met another one.

"That's an interesting story. On the other hand, you could be a thirty-year-old jerk who likes to snoop."

"You remember the time you came to Florida to get the Carousel of Progress? Your father slipped away one evening after dinner, told you to stay in your mecha, told you he had an appointment with someone?" He smiled and smiled, the corners of his mouth curling in on themselves. "We talked all night long. He was very happy with how you were working out, but there were some improvements we agreed we would make in the next generation.

"He loved the Carousel of Progress. It was almost impossible to get him to talk about anything else.

"Your mother—he said you didn't remember her. I do. A great beauty. Smart, too. Acid tongue. She could flay the skin off you at a thousand miles' distance over a mailing list.

"I've followed your career very closely ever since. I felt I owed it to your father. Lost you for a while, but you turned up again in an Indian gentleman's research notes, a gentleman from the IIT. Chandrasekhar.

"He had certain novel theories about transcription. As this is my area of specialty, I paid close attention. Given what I knew of your design, I could tell that his ideas wouldn't apply. On the other hand, I also knew something that you never suspected: Chandrasekhar's little friends in your bloodstream were also gathering a copy of your genome for someone else's use. Don't know if old Race Car was in on it or not, but I wouldn't put it past him. Dude's always been jealous of my mad genomic skills.

"But it's no coincidence that the Midwich plague came along within a few years of you taking the cure. Those little bastards are spreading around the world like a pandemic."

I forgot about the tea. The cooker shrilled at me a few times, but I couldn't do anything about it. I was transfixed.

This guy clearly knew things that I'd wondered about all my life, like my operating parameters, like my parents' life histories, like what happened to Detroit, like who made the youth gangs. The cooker shut itself off.

He laughed. His laugh was the oldest thing about him. It was positively ancient and there wasn't a single nice thing about it. It snapped me back to myself.

"Why?" I said.

"Why what?" The corners of his mouth curled another notch.

"Why are you here now? Why have you been watching me? Why haven't you come before? Just—*why?*"

"How about that tea?" He stood up and helped himself. He took a sip. "Delicious. More like consommé than tea, though." He took another sip, looked out into the night. "I was pretty bummed when you took the cure. I could see where it was going to go. You were our little group's proudest moment, you know, the pinnacle of our achievement. I could tell from looking at Chandrasekhar's publications that it wasn't going to work out. I could also read the writing on the wall: someone was going to get hold of our work and set to work improving it.

"You're the only one, you know. As you might imagine, experimental verification of immortality is a long-term process, not the kind of thing you can do in a hurry. The plan was to let you run for a half century or so before the rest of us had our own kids." He laughed again, that old laugh. "Pretty silly to think that there'd be anything recognizable left after fifty years. It's easy to believe you understand the future just because you've got a reasonable handle on the present, I guess.

"The raid on Detroit was about getting you, you know—your genome, anyway. Originally the plan had been to seduce you, but that wouldn't have gotten your whole genome, just the zygotic half you left behind. Anyway, it was irrelevant because the Treehuggers weren't about to let their daughter be deflowered by an inhuman monster. So instead, they raided you. Your father died to keep you safe. Then what do you do with that legacy? Piss it away because you don't like your protracted adolescence. You would have aged eventually, you know. If all had gone according to plan. You were impatient, and now, well, look at you. You're certainly paying the price for it, aren't you?"

"Leave." I hadn't known that that was what I was going to say until I said it. Once I said it, I said it again. "Leave. Now." I was seeing red. How dare he blame me for what happened to me?

He laughed and that didn't endear him to me at all. "Oh, Jimmy. You're letting your ego get ahead of your good sense again. You needn't be condemned to repeat the mistakes of the past, you know. You can choose otherwise.

"I haven't answered one of your questions yet. Why now? Because I can reverse it. I can undo what Chandrasekhar did. It's my area of specialty, after all. I can make you young again."

"Leave," I said. I didn't believe him for a moment.

He laughed. "I'll come back later, once you've had a chance to think it over."

○ ○ ○

The next day, climbing into my mecha hurt more than usual. The heat arrived early that day, so I woke up in a sweat. The tree's sap-tap yielded sweet water that was already sickly warm, but I drank cup after cup of it before suiting up. It could keep me going all day. I barely looked at my room as I left it, not wanting to see the two cups by the sink, the evidence that I hadn't dreamt my visitor in the night.

The mecha's cargo pouch bulged with my week's foraging: irregular lumps of concrete that still betrayed a few human-made, razor-sharp edges, angles you just couldn't find anymore in a post-wumpus world; half a steel-belted radial that had rested under a rock where the wumpuses had missed it; and the great prize, a whole bag of tampon applicators, what the locals called "beach whistles," discovered in a dried-out septic tank up on Little Duck Island.

This was my living: collecting the junk of our erased civilization. I knew an assemblage sculptor who'd pay handsomely for it in processed cereals, refined sugars, and the other old evils that were nearly impossible to derive from the utopian plants that sprouted all around us. There were sweet edible flowers you could put in your tea, there were mushroom loaves that tasted like whole-grain bread, but there weren't any Twinkie bushes or cigarette trees.

The thing about the main road is that you can see down it for a long, long way, so theoretically it should be hard for the youth gangs to stage an ambush. And the old roadbed was kept smooth by the passage of feet, yielding a less bumpy ride in the mecha, which was a comfort to my old bones.

I stayed away from the road from a little before dusk to a little after dawn. The youth gangs grew more fearless then—or so it seemed to me—and they owned all the high-traffic routes after dark.

But it's not a hard-and-fast rule. That day, they surrounded me on the road, moving like they were on casters, that same eerie precision. It had been five years since I last met a youth gang in the woods at the eve of the militia's dissolution, but I still recognized these kids. They were the same kids—not just similar looking, the same kids, I'd never forget their faces.

They hadn't aged a day.

Again, I rotated my mecha at the waist, looking at each in turn. They met my gaze calmly.

They were filthy now, so grimed that they were all the same mottled brown and green. One appeared to have fungus growing on his shirt. Two were barefoot. They looked like they needed a parent to sit them down and bathe them and put them in a new suit of clothes. And administer a spanking.

I found the one I'd chased to his hidey hole, the one who'd moved with so much preternatural grace and agility. I gave the mecha his scent, told it to track him, only him, to grab him, no matter what. Then I spun a little around, looking a different one in the eyes, hoping to trick them all about the focus of my attention.

They each raised an arm in unison and tried to mindrape me. The headache returned, the same headache, bookmarked and reloaded five years later, and I slapped at the activator control as it descended. *Fetch*, mecha, *fetch!*

The mecha lurched and spun and grabbed, in a series of clicks and thuds. I'd told it to put itself into relentless pursuit mode, without any consideration for me. I heard one of my ribs snap and gasped. That old rib was the same one that had snapped all those years ago.

The headache disappeared, swallowed by the pain in my chest. I heard and felt the rib-ends grating, had a momentary vision of the sharp rib-end punching through my lung. The mecha would be my grave. It would chase the boy and catch him or not, and I would bubble out my last bloody breaths, immortal no longer.

But we were lurching too hard for me to spend time on these visions. The boy was running and dodging through the jungle, again choosing his route based on the mecha's limitations, the places it couldn't leap or smash through. I took over the controls and added my smarts to the mecha, trying to model the boy's behavior and guess where he would go next.

There, he was going to jump into that swampy patch and pull himself out along that old rotting log. So, coil the legs and spring, aiming for the log, doubling over in the air and grabbing for him. Little fucker wasn't going to generation gap me again.

I did it, roared into the air and roared at the pain in my ribs. Caught him on the first bounce. Wrapped my hands around his skinny chest, turned him right side up, and held him in front of my faceplate.

He was eerily calm. I could feel him trying to work his way into my head, his SQUID battering my mind. I flipped on my PA.

"Cut it out," I said. I was breathing hard, each inhale agony from my ribs. "Why can't you little creeps just leave me alone?"

"Jimmy," he said. "What have you done to yourself?"

He spoke in my father's voice.

∘ ∘ ∘

I think I blacked out for a while. I don't know how long I was out, but then I was back and he was just disappearing into another hidey hole, his scrap of a shirt still caught in my mecha's fist. I grabbed for him, but the pain in my ribs nearly made me black out again.

I switched on the mecha's medical stuff and let the needles and probes sink into me while I set the inertial tracker to backtrack—gently—to home. I could see my artist friend some other time and do my trade.

The man with the rings and necklaces and the dandelion clock of hair was waiting for me when I got back.

"That was some chase-scene," he said, as I pried myself out of my tin can.

"Hand me my canes," I gasped, stepping onto the wide limb that led into my treehouse.

He shook his head as he did so. "You don't look so good."

"You want to tape up my ribs?"

"Not especially," he said. He rummaged in his pack and then tossed me something. "Compression shirt. Just put it on and let it do its thing."

In the end, he had to help me into the t-shirt, which was snug and electric blue. It gradually tightened itself around me, like a full-body hug. He showed me how to get it to loosen up for later when I wanted to take it off. I slumped onto my bed.

"What have you done to yourself?" he said.

"You're the second person to ask me that today."

"Yeah, I heard."

"You've been following me, huh?"

He pointed to the sky. "Midges," he said. "My familiars. I have millions of them, all around these parts. They keep me filled in on all the doings on my territory."

"Your territory."

"I'm the shaman of the southland, son. You should be honored. Most people don't even know I exist. I've come to you twice."

"You said you could reverse this," I said, gesturing with my skeletal, liver-spotted arm.

"I said that. It's not hard, really. Just need to send a kill signal to Chandrasekhar's bots and your cells' natural robustness will kick in, lengthening your mitochondria. Once it reaches critical length, bam, you'll just grow back into the boy we programmed you to be."

"I want to stop at eighteen," I said. "That was a good age."

He nodded sagely. "Might take the last couple thousand years off your life, you know."

"How many will that leave me with, though?"

"Oh, *lots*," he said. "I mean, not into the stelliferous period when the stars grow cold, but put it this way: plate tectonics will have rendered the Earth's continents unrecognizable."

"I thought you said that it took a long time to judge the success of immortality?"

"I've got really good models. Lots of compute power these days, if you know where to look."

"All right then, do it. Make me young."

"Ah, there's a little matter of payment, see? Always pay for what you get. There's no other way to run a world." His smile curled in and in, the dimples multiplying.

"I have half an old tire I could let you have," I said,

shrugging and slumping back into my bed. "I guess you could have the mecha, once I'd recovered."

He nodded. "Mighty generous of you. But I had something else in mind: a favor."

I closed my eyes, knowing that this was going to be bad.

"It's those kids. You heard what the one you caught said to you. He's not himself anymore. The Midwich virus turns kids into harvesters for a vast upload-space where models of the consciousness of billions of humans exist in a hive-mind."

"They do what now?"

"They steal your mind and put it in a big computer."

"Why?"

"Because they're programmed to. Whoever designed the Midwich virus wants them to. The second wumpus war was the same thing. Those human-attacking wumpuses were scanning and copying the humans they ate. I think that the Midwich hive-mind has assimilated the wumpus-mind, but I don't know for sure. Maybe they're rivals."

"But *why?*"

He shrugged. "You know the answer. We both do. They do it because someone thought it would be cool. The line between thought and deed is pretty fine these days."

"And why me?"

"Jimmy," he said, sounding disappointed. "You know the answer. You're not stupid. You're our superhuman. Start acting like one. Why you?"

"Because the youth gangs have no effect on me?"

"Yes. And?"

"Because they're derived from me, somehow?"

"Yes. And?"

"Because my father is in there, somehow?"

"Yes. That's a weird one, isn't it? We all assumed he was dead. Maybe he was in cold storage, awaiting scanning. Maybe they scanned him right away."

"What do you want of me?"

"That part's easy," he said.

○ ○ ○

I'd spent so much time ducking youth gangs, but now I was actively seeking them out. Perversely, I couldn't find them. I stuck to the main roads, ranging up and down the keys, letting the mecha drive itself while I kept my eye out for them.

It was one of those perfect days on the keys, when the sky was a cloudless blue to forever, the air scented with delicious, wet jungle smells. I took a break and did a little fishing, using the mecha's radar to spot and plot the fish, then diving forward and snapping up a big grouper and cupping it in the mecha's hands while it thrashed. I put it in a refrigerated compartment on one thigh for later. I loved to pack them in mud, build a fire and put them among the coals. It had been a long time since I'd had fish. But I'd have something to celebrate tonight.

I jogged up and down the keys some more. I came to the place where I'd run into the youth gang the day before and checked to see if the mecha had still buffered the route it took chasing down my little friend. It had. I set the inertial tracker to rerun it, letting the shaman's brace do the work.

I came to it, an unimpressive hill covered in scrub, the entrance to the cave hidden by branches. I dug at the hill with the mecha's huge hands. It was slow going.

An hour later, I had barely made a dent in the hill, and I still hadn't found any of the kids. The tunnel twisted and dipped around the tree roots.

Fuck it. Once upon a time, my mecha had an enormous supply of short-range missiles, not nearly so smart as the ones on my original beast, back in Detroit, but still able to get the job done. When I walked out of the militia, I had the good sense to fill up my frame, the dozen-by-dozen grid that held a gross of explosives.

Over the years, they'd been depleted. The last couple I'd fired hadn't detonated on contact, but had gone up a few minutes later—luckily I'd had the good sense to keep back of the unexploded munitions.

I backed off from the hill and sighted down the tunnel. The flavors of missile I had left were really antipersonnel, low on heat, high on concussion. I figured that if I could get the missile deep enough into the hillside, the concussion wave would crack it open like an egg.

I fired. And missed. The missile tried valiantly to steer itself into the hole that I'd told it to aim for, but it just wasn't up to it. It screamed into the top of the hill and blew, most of the concussion going up and out into the sky, making an incredible roar that the mecha's cowling did little to dampen. I waited for my head to stop ringing and fired another missile, correcting a little.

This one went true, right down into the tunnel, down and down. I counted one hippo, two hippo, and *whoom*, there was a deep *crump* from down below the mecha and the hill disintegrated into the sky.

It sploded like an anthill in a hurricane, turning into gobs of mud that arced in all directions in a rapidly expanding sphere. Caught in it were flinders of tree-root that stuck to my cowl and slid down slowly. For a moment, I caught a glimpse of the crater I'd made, then two huge trees—something derived from cypresses—topped into it, followed by a great inrush of water from the surrounding water table.

I waded in as the water rushed and swirled and scooped my arms through the soup, looking for evidence of the youth gang that had burrowed there, but whatever evidence there had been was now gone. I'd had visions of the hill opening like a stone, splitting dryly and revealing a neat cross-section of the tunnels inside. I hadn't really thought about the water table.

The mud was sucking dangerously at the mecha's legs. If I got it stuck here and had to abandon it, I'd never be able to walk out of the swamp on my own. I levered myself out of the sinkhole and stepped out into the world. I was covered in mud. The skin of the mecha would shed the dirt eventually, but for now, my shiny metal carapace was covered in disgusting, reeking glop.

I was clearly not going about this right.

I moved back out onto the road and headed for the Sugarloaf Key Bridge. The wumpuses had left the bridges intact—otherwise how would they make their way up and down the keys?—and they were the most conspicuous remaining example of human life in the good old days. It was the bridges that the youth gangs staked out most avidly.

It was there I'd find them.

∘ ∘ ∘

Being covered in mud had its advantages. I crouched under the bridge amid the rocks and made myself invisible. I set the mecha to estivate and recharge its batteries, leaving only its various ears and eyes open.

Before shutting down, I primed my whole remaining missile battery, getting them aimed for fast launch, and recorded a macro for getting myself out of there when the time came, before the bridge could come down around my ears. It would be quite a bounce, but I was prepared to give up a rib or two if that's what it took.

Now it was just a matter of staying alert. I kept thinking about my mouth-watering fish and the feast I'd cook that night, drifting off into mouth-watering reverie. Then I'd snap back to my surroundings, looking back at my screens.

Nothing. Nothing. Nothing.

Then: something.

Gliding out of the wilderness at both ends of the bridge like they were on casters. Silent. Eerie. I waited for them to converge on the center of the bridge before I hit it and quit it.

Ker-*blam!* I barely had time to take satisfaction in the incredible, synchronized splosion of the struts at both ends of the bridge giving way, tossing lumps of reinforced concrete high into the sky. I was in the belly of the mecha as it sprang away, leaping nearly as high, landing with coiled legs, pushing off, somersaulting in mid-air, coming down blam-blam, one foot, two foot, on the remaining section of bridge, snatching out with both hands, seizing a wriggling child in each hand, knocking their heads together and leaping away.

I let the mecha pilot itself for a while as I kept an eye out for pursuit. They'd all scattered when I'd chased them before, but that didn't mean they'd do the same when I *caught* a couple of them.

There they were, giving chase, leaping over obstacles, skittering through the dirt. And ahead—more of them, a dozen of them, gliding out of the bush. A couple hours ago, I hadn't been able to find any of them, now they were boiling out of the underbrush.

I wasn't sure what they could do to my mecha, but I didn't want to find out.

The mecha's arms pumped for balance, flailing the kids' bodies back and forth like ragdolls. I tried to get a look at them. I'd snatched up my little friend and one of his buddies, darker skinned, with longer hair. Both had blood on their faces. Either the missile concussion had done that, or I had, when I'd banged their heads together. Like I said, there's not a lot of fine motor control in those mecha suits.

I was breathing hard and it hurt like hell. Felt like another rib had cracked. Aging was coming on pretty quick.

Here's the thing: the mecha has some pretty heavy guns, regular, old-fashioned projectile weapons. I hadn't fired them much in the line of duty, because wumpuses are missile jobs unless you want to chip away at them all day on full auto. So my clips were full.

I could have sprayed those kids as they came out of the jungle, short, auto-targeted bursts. I'm pretty sure that however immortal the little bastards were, they weren't immortal enough to survive ten or twenty explosive slugs in the chest and head.

Why didn't I shoot the kids? Maybe it's because I knew they were my brothers. Maybe I just couldn't shoot kids, even if they weren't kids. Maybe I could plan a neat little explosion and kidnapping, but not gun down my enemies face to face.

The shaman said he needed the kids brought to him at old Finds Bight in the Saddlebunch Keys. That was pretty rough terrain, jungle and swamp the whole way. But the mecha knew how to get there.

One of the kids was thrashing now, trying to get free. The mecha's gyros groaned and creaked as it tried to compensate for the thrashing and the weird terrain.

I dropped the kid. I only needed one.

I watched him fall in the rear-view as the mecha leapt a hillock and went over double, using its free hand as a stabilizing leg, running like a three-legged dog.

That was when one of the kids came down on my mecha's back, clinging to it. I could see the kid through the cowl, its face completely expressionless as its eyes bored into me.

The youth gang's SQUID needs more than one node to be fully effective—they can't own your mind on their own. But that doesn't mean that one kid is helpless. Far from it.

It felt like my head was slowly filling with blood, crushing my brain and making my eyes bug out. Red mist crept around the edges of my vision and blood roared in my ears like the ocean. I couldn't move anything.

I almost smiled. Idiot child. If I couldn't move, I couldn't divert the mecha, and it knew where it was going.

∘ ∘ ∘

"You're the only one that can run this mission," the shaman had said, sitting in my treehouse. "You're the only one they can't just think to death. You might have spoiled your immortality, but that's still intact. You and them, you're all on the same footing. Bring one to me. I'm going to get a login to their little hobby-world. I'm going to blow it wide open.

We'll be able to go there—without having our minds raped by those little pin-dicks."

I didn't exactly black out. My vision contracted to a hazy disc ringed by red-black pulses timed to my heartbeat, and I could barely hear, but I hadn't blacked out. I was still conscious.

So I saw more kids drop onto the mecha's canopy as we galloped toward Saddlebunch. Some slid off when we leapt and jumped, but most stayed on. They had ropes. They lashed themselves down. They did something under the mecha too. Lassoing the legs, it seemed, from the little I could see. Working without any facial expression. Again. Again.

Leaping free, holding onto the ropes. I felt the mecha jerk as the ropes went taut, skidding and tumbling. Then it was up again, running again, on its feet again. Ropes! Inside, I smiled. Idiot kids.

Over the surf-roar of blood in my ears, I heard something else, new sounds. Clattering. The ropes. Something tied to the ends of the ropes.

The mecha jerked again, caught up short.

Anchors, that's what it was. The mecha twisted from side to side, incidentally dislodging the child who stared at me through the carapace. The red haze receded, my muscles came back to me, and I leapt to my controls.

I swung the mecha back upright to give me more maneuverability and put my fingers on the triggers of all four guns. I rotated around to target the anchors behind me. A couple rounds severed the tight ropes. The kid who'd ridden my carapace was just getting to his feet beside the mecha. Another rattle of the guns took care of him, and he burst open.

This is weird, but I'd never shot any person before. I'd blown up wumpuses and taken out the mechas and their drivers in Detroit, but I'd never done *this* before. There was an immediacy to the way he twisted and fell, the way his lungs opened out like wings from the hole the slugs tore in his back. It froze me just as certainly as the child had.

That freeze gave the rest of them the chance they needed. They surrounded me, gliding out of the woods like they were on rollers. Dozens of them. Dozens and dozens of them. I reached for the controls, trying to set the mecha back on its automated path to the shaman. My finger never made it.

There was a blinding headache. It grew and grew, like a supernova. I didn't know how it could hurt more. It hurt more.

It is possible to mindrape an immortal, I discovered, if you don't care about the immortal's mind when it's all over.

PART 4: TURN BACK, TURN BACK

Dad handed me the delicate hydraulic piston, still warm from the printer.

"You know where this goes, right?" He was sweating in the June heat. Keeping all of Comerica Park air conditioned, even with the dome, was impossible, especially during one of those amazingly wet midwestern heat waves.

"I know, Dad," I said. "I can fix this thing in my sleep, you know."

He smiled at me, then switched to a mock frown. "Well, I *used* to think that, but given your recent treatment of one of my prize machines—" He gestured at the remains of the big mecha, blasted open in the Battle for Detroit.

"Oh, Dad!" I said. "What did you *want* me to do? Let them raid us? You know, I took down *eight* of them. Single-handedly."

The flea bounced me, landing on my shoulders and leaping away. I staggered and would have dropped the piston, had Dad not caught me. "You had some help," he said.

He gave me a hug. "It's OK, you know. You were brave and amazing. I love you."

"I love you, too," I said. It was awkward saying it, but it felt good.

"Good," he said. "Now, back to work, you! I'm not paying you to stand around."

"You're paying me?"

"When was the last time you paid rent? You're getting it in trade."

The Carousel sat in the middle of the field, where second base had been. We'd dug it in, sitting it flush to the ground, the way it was supposed to be. It looked great, but it made reaching the maintenance areas a bit of a pain, so we'd winched out the entire Jimmy's Bedroom assembly and put it on the turf next to the Carousel.

Poor Jimmy. One of his arms hung to one side, jerking spastically when I powered him up. I unbuttoned his shirt, fumbling with the unfamiliar fasteners, and undressed him. The arm hydraulics were not easy to get at. Man, screws sucked. I tossed them in the air as I got them free, letting Ike and Mike fight to snatch them out of the sky.

"Aren't you afraid you'll lose one?"

I looked up from my work. Lacey looked prettier than ever, wearing a sleeveless shirt and a pair of shorts that showed off her hips, which had really changed shape in the past couple months, all for the better.

"Jeez," I said. "Don't sneak up on me like that, OK?"

She gave me a playful shove and I shoved her back and then she snuck me a kiss. I broke it off.

"Not in front of my dad," I said, pleading.

"Your dad adores me, don't you, Harv?"

I turned around and there he was, wiping his hands on his many-pocketed work-shorts, then tugging his shirt out of his belt-loop and pulling it on. "You'll do," he said.

I set down the piston carefully.

It sank a few inches below the surface. I tried to pretend it hadn't happened.

Pepe flew over us, then swooped in for a landing. His aim was off, though. He swooped right at my chest. Right *through* my chest.

"Dammit," I said.

"It's OK," Lacey said. "They'll fix it. Let's go for a walk."

"I can't," I said. "I just can't do it. If the spatial stuff isn't working, I can't believe it."

"Debugging is a process. We'll file a bug against it. They'll have it fixed soon enough."

"Look," I said. "If the platform is so buggy that it can't even keep track of collisions, how do we know it's running *us* accurately?"

"Of course it's not running us accurately," she said. "Otherwise, you'd still hate my guts, your dad would still be dead"—Dad nodded—"and you'd be like four hundred years old. Can't you just be happy for once?"

"You keep telling me that things will get better—"

"So forget about a great big, beautiful tomorrow, Jimmy," Dad said. "Maybe they'll never debug it. But tell me that now isn't the best time of your life."

I tried to argue. I couldn't. Whether that was because there was a bug in me, or because he was right, I couldn't say.

CREATIVITY VS. COPYRIGHT

(Newly revised and condensed from his historic address to the 2010 World Science Fiction Convention in Melbourne, Australia)

THERE ARE THREE THINGS I want to cover in this talk. I tell you that because that way you'll know how close I am to the end, as I will tell you each time I get to one of them.

Starting with the first: Anytime someone puts a lock on something that belongs to you and doesn't give you a key, that lock is not there for your benefit. The lock I'm talking about here of course is digital rights management, or DRM—the so-called digital locks that are used to restrict copying and use of digital works. If you've ever bought a DVD from elsewhere that doesn't play here in Australia, if someone's ever given you a game that wouldn't play in your game player, if you've ever gotten a movie and found that you couldn't move it from one device to another, you've experienced DRM.

The biggest lie ever told to creative people is that DRM is there to help them and that it will contain their losses due to piracy. What DRM does primarily is stop authors and creators and publishers from authorizing audiences to follow them to new platforms.

Let me unpack that a little. Most countries—including Australia, since the U.S.-Australia Free Trade

Agreement—have a law that prohibits breaking digital rights management technology, even if you're not committing a copyright infringement. So, for example, if you bought a copy of your own work from Apple or Amazon or any other of the main DRM vendors, you yourself as the owner of that copyright can't remove the DRM without their permission.

This obviously has no nexus with protecting copyright. We usually grant copyright to people who create things, not to corporations whose contribution to the enterprise is making electronics in Chinese sweatshops. But this is a way that copyright moves from creators to distributors. Practically what it amounts to is a way to lock creators into distribution platforms. Take the iPad or the Kindle or any of the other DRM platforms for distributing electronic books. If I were to sell a million dollars worth of eBooks through the iPad, all with DRM on it, I couldn't authorize you, my reader, to follow me to, say, the Kindle. It's as if every time you bought a book at Borders, you were locked into only shelving it in an IKEA bookcase. If you wanted to sell your books through the local independent bookseller down the road, your readers would have to throw away all the books they had bought and buy new copies to shelve on their new bookcases. Or maintain separate parallel libraries where their books would be shelved either on one case or another depending on whose DRM was on it.

This is clearly not useful for creators. Rather, this is a way that the negotiating leverage between the creators and distributors can be tipped toward distributors. So it ends up being used as a club with which to beat creators and the publishers of creative works.

For example, take the iPad or the iPhone, where the likelihood of any one app author getting rich is very small. One of the things Apple likes to tout is the success of the platform. Yes, there are hundreds of thousands of apps for the iPad and the iPhone, and there are millions of apps sold. But when you divide the second number by the first, you come out with an average that tells you that most app authors are making very little money. While a few have gotten rich, the majority of people who create for that platform don't make much at all. But they can't afford to go somewhere else without risking alienating all their customers. Because when they switch to, say, selling their apps on Android (where you might get a larger percentage of the money that the audience spends) you have to be willing to risk that your own customers will abandon their investment in the iPad or iPhone app and buy it again from Android. You're kind of locked into Apple.

As a result, Apple gets to set terms that authors tend not to like. For example, they take 30 percent (ouch!) and they have a very rigorous set of contractual terms that amount to censorship. They prohibited a dictionary because it contained dirty words. They prohibited the Pulitzer Prize–winning editorial cartoons of Mark Fiore because they disparaged public figures. They prohibited a comic book adaptation of James Joyce's *Ulysses* because it had penises in it.

In each of these cases, Apple backed off after a lot of public ridicule. This is free speech—provided enough people are offended enough when you are censored that they'll take up your cause and make the company that censored you feel stupid.

While no publisher is obliged to carry your works, usually there's multiplicity of publishers you can shop your works to. But not if you are locked into one platform or store.

The reason that DRM is a really bad deal for artists and developers of art is not just that it locks us into these platforms, but that it locks us in without delivering what it's supposed to deliver. What we're supposed to get out of the DRM bargain is that if we allow our works to be locked up by distributors, in exchange they'll make sure our works aren't copied. As a technical matter, this has been a complete failure. It has never really worked. Every computer scientist and cryptographer who *doesn't* work for a DRM vendor will tell you that it will *never* work. The only engineers who will tell you it's possible to make computers worse at copying are those who have a direct financial stake in selling you technology to make computers worse at copying.

Fundamentally the entertainment industry put out an RFP (request for proposals) for magic beans. They wanted magic beans that would make computers worse at copying. Anytime you say we have an unlimited budget to spend on magic beans, you will find magic bean vendors. That doesn't mean the magic beans will work, right? The War on Terror precipitated hundreds of RFPs for magic beans that would automatically detect terrorists or automatically prevent airplanes from being blown up. And lo and behold, there were hundreds of people showing up with magic beans to sell to the military-industrial complex. The entertainment complex has found itself with unlimited magic bean vendors as well. So that's the reality. The nonideological, empirical, fact-based reality is that all DRM is broken as soon as anyone decides it's worth breaking.

Every lock can be picked, especially if it's sitting in the lock-picker's living room, or computer. DRM designers know this, but what do they care? They're selling magic beans.

Publishers and distributors know this too. They're not stupid. They're not actually interested in slowing or stopping copying, they're interested in getting the legal protection that stops copyright holders from going to their competitors. For example, when Apple shipped the iPad they shipped it with a DRM that was supposed to stop the piracy of iPad apps. That DRM lasted all of twenty-four hours; they weren't even trying. What they wanted to secure was not the app but their control over the app. The DRM gave them the right to call on the infinite might of the state to intervene on their behalf should anyone try to compete with them and offer a better deal to their authors.

So extending these legal locks ends up decreasing every artist's individual negotiating power with distributors.

Extending copyright does the same thing between creators and publishers. One example is the extension of copyright over sampling. Copyright didn't use to cover sampling—only verbatim copying or certain kinds of derivative works. Samples were considered a legal gray area. Most legal scholars thought they would come under fair use in the United States. Then the courts explicitly extended copyright over sampling.

But sampling has always been a part of creation; there's a reason they call Brahms's First Symphony "Beethoven's Tenth." Artists have been quoting one another as long as they've been making music; listen to the great jazz solos of Charlie Parker. If they had to get a license every time they wanted to quote a snatch of music, then music as we know it wouldn't exist. Sampling has always been integral to the production of music, all the way down to rock 'n' roll. *Sgt. Pepper*, *Pet Sounds*, the great concept albums are all built around this kind of reference sampling, clipping out, remaking. It's part of our music ecosystem.

Then, in the name of protecting artists, we created this exclusive right to license (i.e, control) samples. Artists who sign label deals generally sign over the copyrights to their works to the labels, which means that if you want to sample music you don't go to the artist but you have to deal with the label. If you are signed to one of the big four, a phone call will usually do it. "Bob, this is Fred, remember that deal we did last week when you sampled one of my artists? Well now one of my artists is sampling one of yours. I'm just going to change the names in the contract and send it back to you." So it's trivial. But if you're an indie artist, it's either difficult or impossible. No one will even take your call.

And when you add to this the recent expansion in the length of copyright, you end up with a situation where practically every sound that you may want to sample, virtually everything ever recorded, is owned by one of four companies. Which essentially means that you have to put yourself in harness to one of these labels in order to work in any one of the several genres of music that involves sampling. Or you have to break the law. So that's part one.

Part two, the second point here, which I sometimes grandiosely call Doctorow's Second Law, is that "it's hard to monetize fame but it's impossible to monetize obscurity." As Tim O'Reilly very famously said, "The problem for most artists isn't piracy, its obscurity." It's a great sound bite as things go, but merely being well-known doesn't guarantee that you earn a living. The fact is, most artists have never earned a living. Never have and never will. There's never been an economy that rewards every artist who wants to make art with enough money to go on and make it. This has never been a feature of any civilization. I'm not celebrating this. It's just the fact. Yet people continue to make art anyway.

I think about science fiction when I think about this. Science fiction had its heyday as short stories in the 1930s and 1940s—the pulp days, when the magazines were paying one to two cents a word. If you sent a manuscript off on Monday, you might get it accepted on Wednesday. (This was when the American Post Office worked incredibly fast, almost at the speed of e-mail today.) The check you got on Friday that would pay your rent for the month. Today science fiction magazines pay two to six cents a word; in 1930-adjusted pennies, that's a fraction of a fraction of a cent per word.

The last time I asked an editor of one of the major New York magazines how many stories she was getting a month, she said about a thousand. And she buys about two. So it's clear that this is not a rational economic industry like, say, shoemaking. If your grandfather was a shoemaker and every time he fixed a pair of shoes he got enough money to pay the rent, and there was only one other shoemaker on his road, he was able to support his family. Flash forward two generations and you're still in the family business, except there's 999 other shoemakers on your road and every time you fix a pair of shoes you get enough money to buy a stick of gum. You'd probably find another job.

But the artist or the writer doesn't. Approximately speaking, anyone who can write and sell a short story to *Asimov's* magazine could be writing ad copy for a salary with benefits and a retirement plan. So if the reason you're in the arts is for money, you're really in the wrong business. And the dismal rate for short fiction and poetry and novels (and handmade jewelry and oil paintings done by street vendors) has almost nothing to do with copyright.

I heard a poet speak at a European Union copyright event a couple years ago bemoaning the terrible state of poets' lives, talking about how hard it was to make a living writing poetry. I completely sympathized until she concluded: "That's why we need to defend copyright!" And that's where I broke with her, because even if she had her own special copyright cutlass that allowed her to disembowel people who used her poetry without paying for it, it wouldn't make her an extra penny.

If you really want to make life better for artists, improve their leverage with their publishers. I speak of publishers in the broadest sense here, including record labels and film distributors. Publishing is the job of making the work public: that is to say, identifying a work, identifying an audience for that work, and taking whatever steps necessary to introduce the audience to the work. Sometimes money changes hands and sometimes it doesn't. But that's really what publishing comes down to.

Now some of that artists can do for themselves. But there's an enormous amount of it that's beyond the grasp of an artist, that requires an institution. Even if you're the most organized person in the world (and not all artists are), you don't have a sales force, you can't coordinate printers, you can't do all kinds of stuff that publishers can do. Plus, if you're on tour with your book, you're not at home writing another, and you're also not at the Frankfurt Book Fair selling your book to foreign editors. All that is stuff publishers perform for us. So this is why it's a good partnership when it works.

But there's another version of combining knowledge with special abilities that has a reverse effect; it actually reduces the author's bottom line. For example, your publisher might sew up all the distribution so that if you want to get a book into a bookstore you have to do a deal with him. That's happened periodically in the history of bookselling. And that's happened regularly in the history of music and film distribution. And when all commerce is controlled by a small cartel, people who produce into that supply chain end up suffering.

The music industry is a textbook example of what happens when all the copyrights accrue to a small number of companies, which as a result end up with control over the whole distribution and retail chain.

Say you are signed to a label (and you have to be signed to a label if you want to do things like sampling and not get sued into a wet spot on the pavement) that sells through the iTunes store, and that looks like a good deal for the artist.

For the consumer, not so good. When iTunes, Apple, sells you something as a listener, they actually don't sell it to you—they license it to you. That's what that twenty-six thousand words of boilerplate you have to click through is all about. It's not like lawyers write twenty-six thousand-word license agreements to let you know you have more rights than you thought you had. It's to let you know that they have the right to come over to your house and eat all your food and punch your grandmother and make long distance calls.

The upshot is that it's a license. You as the listener haven't bought it the way you bought a CD or a record. You can't sell it, you can't loan it, you can't give it away, and you sure as hell can't copy it.

This is the business model for digital music: nobody gets to own anything ever again. For the artist, it looks great, because the standard record deal states that if it's a license you get 50 percent of the take, and if its a sale you get a 7 percent royalty. But in reality you end up getting 7 percent because the record company classes this transaction as a "sale" on your royalty statement. The buyer gets treated as a licensor, but for you, the musician, it's a sale, and thus the label pays about six-sevenths less than you're owed. All four of the majors have the same accounting peccadillo, so if you don't like it you can go pound sand. Because who else are you going to license your catalog to? And to add insult to injury, a line item on the standard royalties sheet deducts a certain percentage for "breakage," which apparently accounts for all the bits that are broken on the way to the iTunes store.

This kind of thing gets repeated throughout the other industries where you have strong copyright and a lot of strong copyright lawyers. So, for example, anyone who wants to make a movie that's distributed through the studio system has to go to the insurers that the movie industry has grown up in tandem with, and they insure you against lawsuits for copyright infringement. Before they insure your film, they go through it to make sure you haven't done anything that *might* arise in a lawsuit (not anything that *would* arise in a lawsuit) that they would lose just anything they might get sued for at all. Practically speaking, what that means is if there's someone wearing a t-shirt with a logo on it hanging around in the background of your film, you have to get a license for it.

When I taught at the University of California, I had a student whose summer job was to open checks for the Men in Black franchise. Anyone who shot a movie with a Men in Black comic lying around had to send them a check, not because copyright law said so but because the insurers who work for the studios said so. So when you create obstacles, you create people whose job it is to keep the obstacles in place so they can create problems only they know how to solve. When you use copyright to turn creativity into an obstacle course, you end up giving power to institutions whose job it is to remove obstacles.

It is really only by using policy to remove obstacles to creativity that you end up giving power to creators. This is where we get back to the idea that it's hard to monetize fame but impossible to monetize obscurity. Creative Commons licenses and other tools make it possible for artists to build audiences. YouTube, Twitter, Facebook, etc., allow artists to forge contract with readers or listeners that runs person to person, not person to corporation. (It can be quite exhausting, very asymmetrical: you've got a million readers and there's only one of you, and they all want to send you a tweet, and you have to figure out how to reply to them all! But it sure beats the alternative, which is that you've got no readers and no one gives a tweet.)

This amounts to a social contract, and it's different from an economic contract, in which you only get what you pay for and you only deliver what you gat paid for. The consumer gets the commodity, say, the CD that you get to bring home, and the producer gets the money that you spent on it. You have no responsibility to the producer and the producer has no responsibility to you; you've engaged in an act of commerce, like buying a candy bar, not entering into a relationship.

The artistic business has always had this element of social contract; it's never been merely an economic contract. The artist asks the audience to integrate her art into their lives, to listen to her arguments, to adopt her aesthetic, to hum her tunes to their children, to ruminate on her stories and tell them to themselves—to make her art part of their lives. In return, audiences don't just acquire art, they purchase a part in an artist's career. They feel a stake in it; they promote the art that they love; they do things that run contrary to their theoretical economic interest but that are in favor of their social interest and the interest of the artist that they love. They buy premium items, they buy spare copies, they buy copies just to keep on their shelves; they come out to see authors at festivals. They treat the artist's material as though it were infused with the artist herself or himself.

This isn't the kind of contract that corporations are very good at, which isn't to say don't try. That's why any sentence that contains the word "brand" is almost certainly bullshit. Because "brand" as it's used in corporate board rooms is a way of fooling the customer into feeling as if she's entered into a social contract, while carefully ensuring that there is no reciprocal contract on the part of the corporation. The customer is meant to tirelessly promote and support the brand, but the brand has no duties to the customer; it can even sue the customer for promoting the brand in a way that runs contrary to the brand identity endorsed by the brand's owner.

A world of open networks and social systems is one in which artists get more leverage; in which they can take on some of those very difficult tasks of publishing and building an audience, face fewer bottlenecks, pay less to do more, and get better deals from their publishers. This isn't any guarantee that an artist will earn a living—I'll say it again: most artists will never earn a living—but rather this is a way that ensures when art is bought and sold more of the money that results from those transactions goes to the artist.

And now we're on to the final piece of the puzzle, which is that information doesn't want to be free, people do. In 1985 at the first Hackers' Conference in Silicon Valley, Stewart Brand uttered his famous aphorism, "Information wants to be free; information [also] wants to be expensive." And this was a lovely Zen summation of what was about to happen in the next fifteen years, when information technology would make it easier to copy stuff, but also raised the value of the stuff that was getting easier to copy. And these two trends were to rub up against each other in very interesting and at times catastrophic ways.

This was a very prescient thing for him to have said, but not a moral statement about whether copying is good or bad, and certainly not the ideological basis for people who support copyright reform it has become. "Information wants to be free" has about the same relationship to the copyright fight that "Kill Whitey" has to the civil rights movement or bra burning has to feminism—which is to say that it's a kind of intellectually dishonest cartoon that allow you to duck the real questions and just address the straw man.

And "information wants to be expensive" means that artists and creators often end up taking the stance that either government or corporations have a duty to figure out how to make computers *worse* at copying. This is a fool's errand that will have no measurable effect on "piracy," because copying is as hard now as it is ever going to get, which is not very hard. It's not like next year hard drives are going to become more expensive, or fewer folks will know how to sit down at a computer and type in "Batman Returns bittorrent." From here on in, copying just gets easier.

It's also a fool's errand because it has very negative external effects on society as a whole. In addition to increasing the power of intermediaries over artists (as we see with DRM), it also rewrites the operating system of the information age to build in censorship, surveillance, and control. So, for example, we are creating these national firewalls—as here in Australia, with the aim of ending child pornography, even though the people who make the firewalls say that they won't work for that!

You all know Chekhov's first law of narrative, which is that if you put a gun onstage in act one, someone is going to use it by act three. So once you build a national firewall, everyone who knows of something on the Internet they'd prefer their fellow citizens not see, starts showing up in the halls of government saying we should add this and that to the firewall. In the UK there is a proposal to add trademark and copyright infringement to the national firewall. The same proposal has been floated in the United States and in Ireland and Scandinavia as well.

The problem is, the sites that contain "infringing" material also contain an astounding amount of noninfringing material placed there by artists as part of their legitimate distribution schemes. Take a site like YouTube, with something like a billion files (and about 5 percent of them infringe copyright), which assembles and makes public a body of creative work that is larger than ever dreamt of before. Shut it down? It's as if we've discovered a town that houses the largest library ever built, surrounded by a shantytown of pirated DVDs, and so we propose to bulldoze the whole city.

Everybody gets in on this act, even people who are theoretically progressive and involved in social-justice causes. Last year, Bono from U2 wrote an op-ed in the *New York Times* saying we must end copyright infringement on the Internet. Build a Great Firewall like the one in China, he says. First of all, he's wrong. China, which has the power to arrest you and harvest your organs for high-ranking party members, hasn't managed to build an effective firewall. But even if they could, the idea that Bono is aligning himself with the Chinese government and their tactics in order to control information flow is astounding. I mean, we know you love freedom, we just wish you'd share, Bono!

What happens when you start to control how these networks work is that you need to preemptively examine all the work that goes there. What you end up doing is raising the cost of hosting material altogether. When I spoke at Google Zurich in last year, I said there's about ten hours of video uploaded to YouTube every minute. (I'd gotten that stat about a month before.) A person who worked at YouTube put her hand up and said, "No, it's twenty-nine hours." That was then: now, it's probably like a quintillion hours uploaded every minute.

So if you say to Google, you have an affirmative duty to ensure that none of this stuff infringes copyright before the public is allowed to see it, you fundamentally say to them we expect you to hire an army of copyright lawyers booking more lawyer hours than exist between now and the heat death of the universe. Which is to say, it's impossible.

If you expect Google to watch everything that goes on YouTube before it goes live, something has to give. My guess is, they would solve that problem by restructuring YouTube so that it looks like cable TV. Nothing goes on cable TV until a lawyer and an insurer have signed off on it. In some very lucky places, there are a whopping five hundred cable channels. Imagine if the Internet only had five hundred websites! And of course if the principle of a duty to review for infringement applies to YouTube, there's no reason it shouldn't apply to a blogger or to Twitter or any other place people are making information available.

This is not just bad for indie artists. You end up blocking efforts to organize political movements or form little league teams or bind together far-flung families, as well as to build free and open serve software and to create encyclopedias and do all manner of amazing things. Once you impose the duty to police what gets posted on user-generated content cites, you have to retain ever-larger amounts of information in case someone is found retrospectively to infringe copyright.

It gets worse. YouTube allows users to set some videos as visible only to family and friends, but Viacom in a recent lawsuit argued that you and I and everyone else should be shut off from that privacy option just in case we were using it not to share pictures of our toddlers but old *Mork & Mindy* episodes. And some digital rights management technology includes spyware that records your Internet doings and secretly smuggles them up to some mother ship that's trying to do behavioral marketing. And worst of all, there's the "three-strikes" law being proposed as part of ACTA, an international treaty that Australia participates in. If you are found guilty of three acts of copyright infringement (with a very lightweight standard of proof before something like a traffic court), they cut off your Internet access; and since most of us share a household, it's collective punishment.

If you swipe a DVD from a shop you get a small fine, or if you've done it hundreds of times maybe you get some community service—but we don't come to your house and say, OK, we're going to cut you off from all the services that deliver freedom of speech, freedom of assembly, freedom of the press, access to tools, communities, and ideas, access to education, and civic engagement.

This not a principle we think of as belonging in the justice systems of enlightened countries. People like me fight for copyright reform not because we're cheap and we want DVDs for free but because, in the name of preventing piracy, corporations and governments are attacking fundamentals like the right to assemble, the right to free speech, the right to operate a free press and the right to organize and work together. Information doesn't want to be free, people do! Artists need to transcend the self-serving, terrorized, crappy narrative that's been fed to us by the copyright industries and recognize that the collateral damage from this doomed effort to reduce copying includes the free society that we all cherish.

And there are organizations that will help us. In Australia there's Electronic Frontiers Australia; worldwide there's Electronic Frontiers Foundation, Creative Commons, and many other organizations that work for a balanced copyright regime that respects all the civil liberties that are part of a free society and also tries to insure that artists can go on earning their livings as well.

So thank you and good night.

"LOOK FOR THE LAKE"
CORY DOCTOROW INTERVIEWED BY TERRY BISSON

Let's see if I can make this work. Across a sea and a continent. Oakland to London via Skype. Seems appropriate.

Hey, Cory. I've met you in several of your incarnations: coeditor of Boing Boing, *the hottest site on the web; award winning SF writer;* New York Times *bestselling YA author. Which one am I talking to?*

Any or all of the above. I've been lucky, it's true. But it's complicated. It reminds me of when my grandmother called me up from Florida and said, "My friends want to know what you do for a living. They don't really understand it." I have that problem every time I fly into the UK and have to fill in a landing card and get it all in eleven letters. Writer, blogger, editor, professor, speaker, hacker, journalist, and so on.

So let's start with Boing Boing. *The first time I checked out that amazing site, I thought, this is all new! And yet (I'm an old-school '60s guy, as you know) it was strangely familiar. Then it came to me: It's the Whole Earth Catalog.*

Absolutely. Access to tools and ideas. I opened up one of my old Whole Earth Catalogs a few years ago and I was like: These are the layouts we use. And here's something else that blew my mind: I was yard-saleing in Burbank and I found a replica of a nineteenth-century Sears Catalog and it reads like *Boing Boing*.

So the Whole Earth Catalog was the Sears Catalog for the '60s?

Yeah, and *Boing Boing* is the electronic version that can change to keep up with shit as it happens. I kind of had a watershed experience in my professional and intellectual life when a friend of mine slipped me a copy of *Whole Earth Review*, which grew out of the original catalog. "The body is obsolete" was the theme of that issue, with articles by a bunch of early transhumanists, and it completely revolutionized my outlook.

I went from there to *Co-evolution Quarterly* to *Mondo2000* to the first issues of *Wired* to downloading Bruce Sterling's article on the best software developers being not well-rounded but being thoroughly spiked. And it's like a straight line, like an arrow, from the day I got that issue of the *Whole Earth Review* to the day I dropped out of university to program for Voyager in New York.

It looks to me like that's what you might call the agenda of your fiction, the project. You're trying to give readers that same kick.

And of my nonfiction as well.

I write fiction because I find it aesthetically pleasing and because I find it artistically satisfying. I like the way the sentences sound and the way the people come to life in my head and on the page. I like to tell stories.

Blogging has a whole different aesthetic. One thing that blogging does for me that nothing else ever did—it creates those synthetic moments when a bunch of things that are seemingly disparate snap together. When you write up material for public consumption, you have to clarify it in your own head, and doing that often makes it connect in new ways. I have a lot of those *aha* moments. Maybe I have five disparate things to write about, and I find this sixth one, and I'm like, "Aha, so this is how they're all related!" And then I rush off and write a book or a short story or an essay about it.

So in a sense *Boing Boing* is the Whole Earth Catalog, arming folks for action and understanding. But it's also a cognitive prosthesis for me, without which I wouldn't be able to write the stuff that I write.

So you're saying Boing Boing *serves as a writer's notebook?*

Even better. You can't cheat a blog the way you can cheat a writer's notebook. I have notebooks that are filled with notes to myself that I wrote in such haste that I can't remember what I meant anymore. You can't do that with a blog.

You were pretty well established as a SF writer when you sort of veered into YA (young adult). How did that come about?

I wouldn't call it veered. It started with Kathe Koja. I'm a big fan of her books, and she was like "country before country was cool." She started doing YA before there was a boom and before it was profitable. I ran into her at a con and she told me about the level of engagement she got from her readers, about how she was meeting up with kids who explicitly read to find out how the world worked. To me, that struck a chord. It reminded me of why I read, not just SF but *everything*. I was one of those reader kids, as you probably were too. And reading was a lot about figuring out about how the world worked. I remember having these *aha* moments, especially reading older SF. "Oh, so *that's* who Woodrow Wilson was. Oh, so that's what the Great Depression was all about!"

I was also hanging out with Scott Westerfeld and Justine Larbalestier and Charlie Stross at that same con.

You know how you meet people that you just *click* with, and you form a little rat-packy group and end up going to all your meals together? Scott talked about this too, this level of engagement with younger readers. Someone else (I thought it was Garth Nix, but he tells me it wasn't) told me that a YA story had all this dramatic potential because when you're young you do a bunch of stuff for the first time. It's like you're jumping off a cliff, over and over. Cliff after cliff. That all resonated with me in a big way.

So you wrote Little Brother.

It cohered in my head, like, overnight. And then literally from that night to the day I finished the first draft was eight weeks.

That velocity certainly carried over. I heard you read from Little Brother *at SFinSF and was jealous as hell. What I liked best was the way you defined the character through the information he carried. You never say what he looks like, but you know all about him because of what he knows and what he wants to tell you. Through info dumps!*

Well *Little Brother* is deliberately expository in that Heinleinian way, and in that sense it's a rule-breaking book. I'm sure you've heard Stan Robinson complain about the Turkey City Lexicon—"no info dumps," "show and don't tell," and so forth. Useful rules for writers, but fun to break as well. Sometimes the most efficient way to get something into the head of your reader is "tell and don't show."

There is an admirable fleetness in taking info that might drag out an otherwise dramatic scene, and just dumping it on the reader; saying, "Got it? Good. Let's go!" Heinlein did that so well in his juvies!

These days a lot of SF writers (and others!) are moving into YA because it's more profitable. But it seems to me that you also have a political agenda. Can say anything about that?

That goes back to what you said earlier, about having a project. I don't have a name for it, but it's about technology and liberation. Those are the words I'd use. My work is all in service to it—the blog, the YA fiction, the technological advocacy, the standards work, the lobbying. All of that stuff is part of a bigger project.

Where YA comes in, I guess, is that kids are never part of the status quo. They are outlaws by hereditary design. Plus they are tuned into technology. And technology always favors the attacker, not the defender.

Cool. So you're arming a constituency that's interested in changing things. You're passing out weapons to the kids.

That's a lovely way to put it. I'm sure that'll read great on my indictment sheet. But it does seem a little like that. The weapons of course are ideas and information. I've thought a lot about what it's like to be an activist in the era of Google. I think it's less important to know facts than it is to know keywords. Keywords are capabilities: if you know something can be done, you can figure out how to do it.

What do you think of WikiLeaks?

That's funny, because the novella I just finished is kind of a WikiLeaks story and I didn't mean for it to be. So that tells me that I have a strong opinion about it.

I think it's important to disambiguate whatever you think about Julian Assange from WikiLeaks. I don't know Julian, I know him only peripherally through some friends. But the story of Julian has taken on a life of its own.

The real story of WikiLeaks is what it is—the total open release of former state secrets. That part is really interesting. I believe that it's meaningful and substantial and game-changing for us to know for a fact, with citable information, some of the nastiness, arm-twisting, and corruption—and there's no word for it except *corporatism*—that takes place behind (formerly) closed doors.

Many of us grow up thinking that we live in a society where governments and corporations more or less behave themselves. But this is so visibly untrue when you go through WikiLeaks! What looks like democracy is really corporations shopping for "the best government that money can buy." Over and over again, our best interests are set aside and auctioned off. WikiLeaks reveals the ways in which our society is corporatist. Maybe not every policy that gets made and maybe not everything is corrupt, but at the end of the day this is the society we live in. This truth is unequivocally powerful.

So on the whole, I think WikiLeaks is generally a force for good. On the other hand, the notion of everything being leaked, everything being leakable, is one we have not yet come to grips with. What happens when it gets personal, not just for the rich and powerful, but for everybody? All the things that are embarrassing or humiliating, all that stuff is just going to start oozing out onto the Internet linked with your name.

So transparency turns into its opposite. An enemy of personal freedom.

It could happen. It could also not happen.

We've had telescopes for a long time but we don't have an epidemic, at least not that I know of, of people using them to spy on their neighbors. There are creepy people who do it, but they're creepy, right? It didn't turn into a social norm that if you haven't put your blinds down you deserve to be peeped. Instead we somehow managed to cling to the idea that you're a dick if you're looking through my window.

That's a morality, an ethic that I hope we can maintain in this surveillance culture. And I do think there's a major difference between exposing the wrongdoings of governments and elected representatives, and governments and elected representatives spying on us, using technology to control us better. Those aren't the same thing.

You went to that Singularity Conference back in 2006. What do you think about the Singularity? The idea that at some point (and soon!) our machines will be smarter than we are?

You know what's funny about that question? I had the first lines of a short story this morning that I tweeted because I didn't know what else to do with it. Let me see if I can find it. It was a very "Bears Discover Fire" first line, if I do say so myself. Here it is:
"Honey, the Singularity is at the door. He says everything is different now."
"Tell him we don't want anything now."
"He's very insistent."

I love it. What happens next?

That's the problem, isn't it? I think the Singularity is a literary device (and also a spiritual belief system) that naturally arises from people who try to imagine a world in which everything gets better and, at the same time, run up against the limits of their imagination in trying to imagine a boundary condition for progress.
What happens when you reach the end of progress?
Well the end of progress, when it all bursts, is the Singularity. Predicting it is one thing, describing it another. It's like when our species developed a theory of mind. I think that someone who has a theory of mind and someone who doesn't probably don't have much to say to each other. But we're trying. Charlie Stross and I are writing a book right

now called *The Rapture of the Nerds*. We stole the title from Ken MacLeod.

I hope I'll still be able to read it when it comes out. Do you go to lots of SF conventions?

I always go to WorldCon. But the con thing is fading, empirically. The numbers are down at almost every con, and the fans who go are getting older. I was a con-going baby fan. When I was fifteen I volunteered at the local convention and slept in the gopher hole, and that was my entre to SF fandom. That was Ad Astra in Toronto, and when I was going, there were like two thousand people, and now there's four or five hundred, and the younger people who are turning up are basically my generation; there's no one behind us. In contrast, the gaming and anime conventions are so orgasmically huge! The interesting thing about them is that almost without exception they were founded by con-going SF fans.

ComicCon, the huge San Diego comics gathering, was started by people like you and me. We would recognize them instantly as part of the tribe. They hit 275,000 before the San Diego fire marshal made them limit memberships. So cons are running, but not our kind of cons. Not the traditional science fiction fan con.

Why do you think that is?

My Tor editor, Patrick Nielsen Hayden, who knows more about this stuff than I ever will, traces the decline back to a conscious decision to exclude a certain kind of celebrity and commerciality from SF cons. In the 1980s, everyone was worried about the Star Trek conventions turning into a kind of velvet-rope deal, with the guests emerging from the green room to see the public, then retreating back into it. And there'd be the good party and the bad party, and you can see why SF, being the literature of outcasts, rejected that. You wouldn't want your thing where everyone belonged to turn into a thing where once again you were sitting at the uncool kids' table.

What happened was that the cons that were run by fans who were willing to integrate a little of that glitzy stuff, like the ComicCon founders, just kind of took off; and the cons that stayed the way they were, didn't.

You went from fan to pro pretty quick, with Down and Out in the Magic Kingdom. *I know you went to Clarion, the famous SF workshop. Do you still workshop stuff, pass it by others before it's published?*

I don't workshop anymore, because I travel too much. I miss it. When my daughter gets a little older, I'm going to go back to my summer workshop, the one we do in Toronto every year. Some of us went to Clarion together, others just got invited in because we knew their work and taste. You bring a story and you write a story and you workshop them all. You learn to look at your work through the eyes of others.

I really like the process but I can't do the week-long workshops. I have too many projects going at once.

Sounds like a good problem to have. How do you keep up with it all?

I set a word target and I just hit it everyday. When I hit that word target I stop. Period. I stop in the middle of a sentence, so I can start the next day without having to think of anything. I don't remember who told me that trick, but I swear to God if there was just one thing I could teach other writers, it would be that.

Wasn't it Hemingway who said that if you stop in the middle, you always start up easy.

Might have been Hemingway. I wouldn't be surprised if it were a Babylonian scribe. Its one of those things that, once you learn it, just feels right. But until you do it, it seems crazy.

What if there were two things?

If there were two things I could teach people, the second would be to write every day. It's the one thing I wish I'd started doing ten years earlier. I always thought, "Every damn day? What are you talking about? I have to lure the muse into the room, how can I write every day?"

But writing every day was transformative. Now it's at the top of my to-do list. I sit down. I put my bum in my chair and I write. When I'm super, super busy or traveling, my target might be as little as 200–250 words a day, which is peanuts. I type 70–80 words a minute. I've got twenty-four hours to think about what those words are going to be. I can write them. So I do.

That was Trollope's method.

So, you see?

How do you keep the plot in mind?

Usually I work from a treatment instead of a plot outline. I know the kind of things that are going to happen, and maybe a few set pieces, but I don't always know how to get from A to B. My rule of thumb, my heuristic for getting from A to B, is to use what I call The Lake. I always try to have the character trying and failing to solve his (or her) problem and for the problems to always be getting worse. It's an Algis Budrys (the SF writer) type of thing. So long as the attempts to solve the problem are intelligent, there's always a reason to turn the page. Because you want to see people who are intelligent trying to solve problems and you can't look away when they're failing and things are getting worse. I think that's almost a pocket definition of dramatic tension.

What the hell does that have to do with a lake?

I grew up in Toronto, which is in a lake basin. The lake is south, so downhill is always south. You can't get lost. Wherever there's a junction, if you just go downhill eventually you get to the lake. And if you just make things get worse for your characters, eventually you get to the end. They solve the problem and the novel ends. There are probably more compact ways of getting there, but you can always get there if things are always getting worse. So you can always get to the lake, if that's where you're trying to go.

Back to Boing Boing. *You cover an awfully wide and wonderfully eclectic variety of stuff. How do you decide what to keep up with? (Not to mention, how do you do it?)*

With a little help from my friends. As a culture, we have gone from a deterministic method of consumption of media to a probabilistic one.

For example, the old SF fans still talk about how you could read the whole field, back in the day. You could read every novel, every magazine, and if you missed something, someone would tell you about it. Deterministic.

Now what happens is that I can't even read all my RSS feeds or e-mails or tweets, much less the novels or events they are about. But the good stuff bubbles up anyway because of reblogging, retweeting, whatever you want to call it. That's what I mean by probabilistic.

Some folks—like the people at the *New York Times* or the *Advertising Age* resident curmudgeon, or that guy at the Columbia School of Journalism who hates my guts—dismiss retweeting, reblogging and such as "parasitic." They don't get it. It is the only way we can have an adequate navigational apparatus for negotiating the sheer volume of material available to us. Without it, there would be no movement from inside your first orbit of social and cultural contacts, no line to the millions who know a million others from a million different walks of life, the cross-pollinators who gets a little bit of information from here and send it there, and connect us all. Without them, the conversation would die. These are the people who are essentially making sure that whatever is locally good for you bubbles up to the top of your pile. They are as important to the future fecundity of media as bees are to the future fecundity of plants.

There is one question I ask everybody. What kind of car do you drive?

I've only owned one car in my life. I owned it for one year, the year I lived in Los Angeles. It was a Hyundai Elantra. A friend who is a car geek told me: "Find a car that's never been in a wreck, that's below its bluebook, and then sell it at the end of the year. It'll be cheaper than leasing." And he was right, I sold it for exactly what I paid it. I covered everything in it in sheepskin as an experiment. Sheepskin steering wheel cover, sheepskin seat covers, and it was like it just oozed lanolin everywhere. I got a horn that played "Low Rider." So that was LA. Now I have an RFID key that gets me a short-hire bicycle. They're all over London, and that's how I get around.

So, back to my original question. When you look in the mirror these days, who looks back? A science fiction writer, a journalist, a teacher, a blogger, an activist?

Depends on the day, or maybe the time of day. I don't spend a lot of time looking in the mirror. I don't sweat that stuff anymore. It reminds me of when we were all generic subculture kids trying on identities. Are you a cow punk? Are you a crusty punk? A hardcore punk? A straight-edge punk? Worrying about what niche you're in is a little too much like high school.

Let's just say you're a Cory Doctorow sort of guy.

BIBLIOGRAPHY

NOVELS

Down and Out in the Magic Kingdom (Tor, 2003)
Eastern Standard Tribe (Tor, 2004)
Someone Comes to Town, Someone Leaves Town (Tor, 2005)
Little Brother (Tor Teens, 2008)
Makers (Tor, 2009)
For the Win (Tor Teens, 2010)
Pirate Cinema (Tor Teens, 2012)
Rapture of the Nerds (with Charles Stross) (Tor, 2012)

GRAPHIC NOVELS

Cory Doctorow's Futuristic Tales of the Here and Now (IDW,
     2008)
Anda's Game (FirstSecond, 2012)

NONFICTION

The Complete Idiot's Guide to Publishing Science Fiction (with
     Karl Schroeder) (Alpha, 2000)
Content (Tachyon, 2008)
Context (Tachyon, 2011)

COLLECTIONS

A Place So Foreign and Eight More (Four Walls Eight
    Windows, 2003)
Overclocked (Thunder's Mouth, 2007)
With a Little Help (Sweet Home Grindstone, 2010)

ABOUT THE AUTHOR

CORY DOCTOROW (CRAPHOUND.COM) IS A science fiction novelist, blogger, and technology activist. He is the co-editor of the popular blog *Boing Boing* (boingboing.net), and a contributor to the *Guardian*, the *New York Times*, *Publishers Weekly*, *Wired*, and many other newspapers, magazines, and websites.

He was formerly Director of European Affairs for the Electronic Frontier Foundation (eff.org), a nonprofit civil liberties group that defends freedom in technology law, policy, standards and treaties. He is a visiting senior lecturer at Open University (UK) and scholar in virtual residence at the University of Waterloo (Canada). In 2007, he served as the Fulbright Chair at the Annenberg Center for Public Diplomacy at the University of Southern California.

In 2008, he became a father. His daughter, Poesy Emmeline Fibonacci Nautilus Taylor Doctorow is a marvel that puts all the works of technology and artifice to shame.

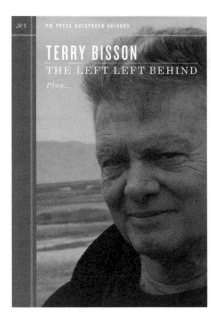

PM PRESS
OUTSPOKEN AUTHORS

The Left Left Behind
Terry Bisson
978-1-60486-086-3
$12

Hugo and Nebula award-winner Terry Bisson is best known for his short stories, which range from the southern sweetness of "Bears Discover Fire" to the alienated aliens of "They're Made out of Meat." He is also a 1960s' New Left vet with a history of activism and an intact (if battered) radical ideology.

The *Left Behind* novels (about the so-called "Rapture" in which all the born-agains ascend straight to heaven) are among the bestselling Christian books in the US, describing in lurid detail the adventures of those "left behind" to battle the Anti-Christ. Put Bisson and the Born-Agains together, and what do you get? *The Left Left Behind*—a sardonic, merciless, tasteless, take-no-prisoners satire of the entire apocalyptic enterprise that spares no one-predatory preachers, goth lingerie, Pacifica radio, Indian casinos, gangsta rap, and even "art cars" at Burning Man.

Plus: "Special Relativity," a one-act drama that answers the question: When Albert Einstein, Paul Robeson, J. Edgar Hoover are raised from the dead at an anti-Bush rally, which one wears the dress? As with all Outspoken Author books, there is a deep interview and autobiography: at length, in-depth, no-holds-barred and all-bets off: an extended tour though the mind and work, the history and politics of our Outspoken Author. Surprises are promised.

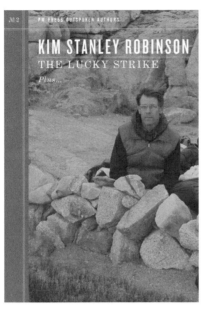

PM PRESS
OUTSPOKEN AUTHORS

The Lucky Strike
Kim Stanley Robinson
978-1-60486-085-6
$12

Combining dazzling speculation with a profoundly humanist vision, Kim Stanley Robinson is known as not only the most literary but also the most progressive (read "radical") of today's top-rank SF authors. His best-selling Mars Trilogy tells the epic story of the future colonization of the red planet, and the revolution that inevitably follows. His latest novel, *Galileo's Dream*, is a stunning combination of historical drama and far-flung space opera, in which the ten dimensions of the universe itself are rewoven to ensnare history's most notorious torturers.

The Lucky Strike, the classic and controversial story Robinson has chosen for PM's new Outspoken Authors series, begins on a lonely Pacific island, where a crew of untested men are about to take off in an untried aircraft with a deadly payload that will change our world forever. Until something goes wonderfully wrong.

Plus: *A Sensitive Dependence on Initial Conditions*, in which Robinson dramatically deconstructs "alternate history" to explore what might have been if things had gone differently over Hiroshima that day.

As with all Outspoken Author books, there is a deep interview and autobiography: at length, in-depth, no-holds-barred and all-bets-off: an extended tour though the mind and work, the history and politics of our Outspoken Author. Surprises are promised.

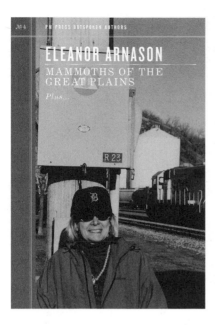

PM PRESS
OUTSPOKEN AUTHORS

*Mammoths of the Great
Plains*
Eleanor Arnason
978-1-60486-075-7
$12

When President Thomas Jefferson sent Lewis and Clark to explore the West, he told them to look especially for mammoths. Jefferson had seen bones and tusks of the great beasts in Virginia, and he suspected—he hoped!—that they might still roam the Great Plains. In Eleanor Arnason's imaginative alternate history, they do: shaggy herds thunder over the grasslands, living symbols of the oncoming struggle between the Native peoples and the European invaders. And in an unforgettable saga that soars from the badlands of the Dakotas to the icy wastes of Siberia, from the Russian Revolution to the AIM protests of the 1960s, Arnason tells of a modern woman's struggle to use the weapons of DNA science to fulfill the ancient promises of her Lakota heritage.

Plus: "Writing SF During World War III," and an Outspoken Interview that takes you straight into the heart and mind of one of today's edgiest and most uncompromising speculative authors.

Praise:
"Eleanor Arnason nudges both human and natural history around so gently in this tale that you hardly know you're not in the world-as-we-know-it until you're quite at home in a North Dakota where you've never been before, listening to your grandmother tell you the world."   —Ursula K. Le Guin

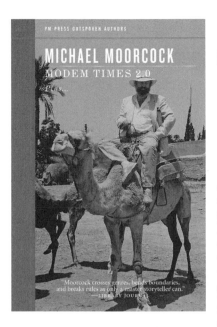

PM PRESS
OUTSPOKEN AUTHORS

Modem Times 2.0
Michael Moorcock
978-1-60486-308-6
$12

As the editor of London's revolutionary *New Worlds* magazine in the swinging sixties, Michael Moorcock has been credited with virtually inventing modern Science Fiction: publishing such figures as Norman Spinrad, Samuel R. Delany, Brian Aldiss and J.G. Ballard.

Moorcock's own literary accomplishments include his classic "Mother London," a romp through urban history conducted by psychic outsiders; his comic Pyat quartet, in which a Jewish antisemite examines the roots of the Nazi Holocaust; Behold The Man, the tale of a time tourist who fills in for Christ on the cross; and of course the eternal hero Elric, swordswinger, hellbringer and bestseller.

And now Moorcock's most audacious creation, Jerry Cornelius—assassin, rock star, chronospy and maybe-Messiah—is back in *Modem Times 2.0*, a time twisting odyssey that connects 60s London with post-Obama America, with stops in Palm Springs and Guantanamo. *Modem Times 2.0* is Moorcock at his most outrageously readable—a masterful mix of erudition and subversion.

Plus: a non-fiction romp in the spirit of Swift and Orwell, Fields of Folly; and an Outspoken Interview with literature's authentic Lord of Misrule.

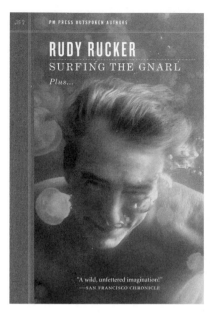

PM PRESS
OUTSPOKEN AUTHORS

Surfing the Gnarl
Rudy Rucker
978-1-60486-309-3
$12

The original "Mad Professor" of Cyberpunk, Rudy Rucker (along with fellow outlaws William Gibson and Bruce Sterling) transformed modern science fiction, tethering the "gnarly" speculations of quantum physics to the noir sensibilities of a skeptical and disenchanted generation. In acclaimed novels like *Wetware* and *The Hacker and the Ant* he mapped a neotopian future that belongs not to sober scientists but to drug-addled, sex-crazed youth. And won legions of fans doing it.

In his outrageous new *Surfing the Gnarl*, Dr. Rucker infiltrates fundamentalist Virginia to witness the apocalyptic clash between Bible-thumpers and Saucer Demons at a country club barbecue; undresses in orbit to explore the future of foreplay in freefall ("Rapture in Space"); and (best of all!) dons the robe of a Transreal Lifestyle Adviser with How-to Tips on how you can manipulate the Fourth Dimension to master everyday tasks like finding an apartment, dispatching a tiresome lover, organizing closets and iPods, and remaking Reality.

You'll never be the same. Is that good or bad? Your call.

FRIENDS OF

These are indisputably momentous times—the financial system is melting down globally and the Empire is stumbling. Now more than ever there is a vital need for radical ideas.

In the three years since its founding—and on a mere shoestring—PM Press has risen to the formidable challenge of publishing and distributing knowledge and entertainment for the struggles ahead. With over 100 releases to date, we have published an impressive and stimulating array of literature, art, music, politics, and culture. Using every available medium, we've succeeded in connecting those hungry for ideas and information to those putting them into practice.

Friends of PM allows you to directly help impact, amplify, and revitalize the discourse and actions of radical writers, filmmakers, and artists. It provides us with a stable foundation from which we can build upon our early successes and provides a much-needed subsidy for the materials that can't necessarily pay their own way. You can help make that happen – and receive every new title automatically delivered to your door once a month – by joining as a Friend of PM Press. And, we'll throw in a free T-Shirt when you sign up.

Here are your options:

 • $25 a month: Get all books and pamphlets plus 50% discount on all webstore purchases.

 • $25 a month: Get all CDs and DVDs plus 50% discount on all webstore purchases.

 • $40 a month: Get all PM Press releases plus 50% discount on all webstore purchases

 • $100 a month: Sustainer. - Everything plus PM merchandise, free downloads, and 50% discount on all webstore purchases.

For those who can't afford $25 or more a month, we're introducing Sustainer Rates at $15, $10 and $5. Sustainers get a free PM Press t-shirt and a 50% discount on all purchases from our website.

Just go to **WWW.PMPRESS.ORG** to sign up. Your Visa or Mastercard will be billed once a month, until you tell us to stop. Or until our efforts succeed in bringing the revolution around. Or the financial meltdown of Capital makes plastic redundant. Whichever comes first.

PM PRESS was founded at the end of 2007 by a small collection of folks with decades of publishing, media, and organizing experience. PM Press co-conspirators have published and distributed hundreds of books, pamphlets, CDs, and DVDs. Members of PM have founded enduring book fairs, spearheaded victorious tenant organizing campaigns, and worked closely with bookstores, academic conferences, and even rock bands to deliver political and challenging ideas to all walks of life. We're old enough to know what we're doing and young enough to know what's at stake.

We seek to create radical and stimulating fiction and non-fiction books, pamphlets, t-shirts, visual and audio materials to entertain, educate and inspire you. We aim to distribute these through every available channel with every available technology—whether that means you are seeing anarchist classics at our bookfair stalls; reading our latest vegan cookbook at the café; downloading geeky fiction e-books; or digging new music and timely videos from our website.

PM Press is always on the lookout for talented and skilled volunteers, artists, activists and writers to work with. If you have a great idea for a project or can contribute in some way, please get in touch.

PM PRESS
PO Box 23912
Oakland CA 94623
510-658-3906
www.pmpress.org